The third man whispered something Fargo didn't catch and the three spread out and converged. Their pistols were out and pointed but they weren't very sure of themselves. They inched forward as if treading on eggshells.

Fargo's natural inclination was to gun them then and there. Instead he said, "That's far enough, gents."

Two froze, but the third spun and raised his revolver. Fargo fanned the Colt and the slug caught the would-be assassin in the chest and smashed him onto his back.

The other two stared as their companion writhed and gurgled and died.

"Are you as stupid as your pard?" Fargo said. "Drop your hardware or the same happens to you."

THE
TRAILSMAN
#392

COLORADO
CARNAGE

by

Jon Sharpe

A SIGNET BOOK

SIGNET
Published by the Penguin Group
Penguin Group (USA) LLC, 375 Hudson Street,
New York, New York 10014

USA | Canada | UK | Ireland | Australia | New Zealand | India | South Africa | China
penguin.com
A Penguin Random House Company

First published by Signet, an imprint of New American Library,
a division of Penguin Group (USA) LLC

First Printing, June 2014

The first chapter of this book appeared in *Night Terror*, the three hundred ninety-first
volume in this series.

 REGISTERED TRADEMARK—MARCA REGISTRADA

ISBN 978-0-451-46803-1

Printed in the United States of America
10 9 8 7 6 5 4 3 2 1

The Trailsman

Beginnings . . . they bend the tree and they mark the man. Skye Fargo was born when he was eighteen. Terror was his midwife, vengeance his first cry. Killing spawned Skye Fargo, ruthless, cold-blooded murder. Out of the acrid smoke of gunpowder still hanging in the air, he rose, cried out a promise never forgotten.

The Trailsman they began to call him all across the West: searcher, scout, hunter, the man who could see where others only looked, his skills for hire but not his soul, the man who lived each day to the fullest, yet trailed each tomorrow. Skye Fargo, the Trailsman, the seeker who could take the wildness of a land and the wanting of a woman and make them his own.

The Rocky Mountains, 1861—two towns wage war and Fargo is caught in the middle.

1

Skye Fargo wasn't expecting trouble. He was high in the Rocky Mountains, camped for the night in a small clearing. His fire had died low and the Ovaro was dozing. He lay on his back with his head propped in his hands and listened to the wavering howl of a far-off wolf.

A big man, broader at the shoulders than most, Fargo wore buckskins and a red bandanna and boots. Unlike some men, he never took his boots off when he turned in for the night. Not in the wilds. A man never knew but when danger might threaten.

Fargo was on the cusp of drifting off when the Ovaro raised its head and nickered. Instantly, he was alert. The stallion was staring toward the rutted road they had been following for the better part of three days. Its ears were pricked and its nostrils flared, and it stamped a front hoof.

Fargo rolled off his blankets and into a crouch, drawing his Colt as he rose. It was pushing midnight. No ordinary traveler would be abroad that late. Only those up to no good.

Working quickly, using his saddlebags and a branch he'd broken for firewood, Fargo rigged his blanket so at a glance it would appear he was asleep. As a last touch he placed his hat where his head would be.

Melting into the shadows, Fargo waited. It could have been hostiles. The Utes weren't happy about having their territory overrun by the white man. Or it could have been highwaymen. Thanks to all the gold and silver strikes that lured pilgrims by the thousands to the mountains, outlaws were as thick as fleas on a hound dog.

Fargo heard footfalls and a whisper. They were clumsy about it. That told him they weren't Utes. No self-respecting warrior would be so careless. By the sounds he counted three.

Fargo had crouched in front of a small pine so his silhouette would blend into the tree's. They didn't spot him. They were intent on his blankets. At the edge of the clearing they stopped, and to

1

Fargo's amusement, one of them was dumb enough to whisper to the others.

"Do you reckon it's him?"

"Has to be. Look at that horse. If that ain't a pinto, I'll eat my spurs."

Fargo's amusement faded. The Ovaro wasn't a pinto, but those who didn't know horses often mistook it for one. Of more interest was the fact that the three lunkheads were after him, specifically. Few people knew he was in that part of the country at that particular time. His mind raced with what it might mean. He had questions, and he wanted answers.

The third man whispered something Fargo didn't catch and the three spread out and converged. Their pistols were out and pointed but they weren't very sure of themselves. They inched forward as if treading on eggshells.

Fargo's natural inclination was to gun them then and there. Instead he said, "That's far enough, gents."

Two froze, but the third spun and raised his revolver. Fargo fanned his Colt and the slug caught the would-be assassin in the chest and smashed him onto his back.

The other two stared as their companion writhed and gurgled and died.

"Are you as stupid as your pard?" Fargo said. "Drop your hardware or the same happens to you."

One man dropped his as if it were a hot coal. "Don't shoot, mister. Please. I ain't hankerin' to die."

The last outlaw hesitated. "You'll kill us anyway."

"Not if you shed that six-shooter," Fargo said.

"I don't believe you."

"Your choice."

The man made up his mind. He dived and fired at where he thought Fargo must have been but he was wide by a yard. Fargo fanned the Colt twice and the body flopped a few times and was still.

"God Almighty!" the man who had dropped his revolver exclaimed, and jerked his arms at the stars. "Please, mister. I have a missus and five sprouts."

Fargo unfurled and warily walked over.

The surviving specimen was in his twenties. He was cockeyed and had a nose that had been busted once and was bent at an odd angle. Tufts of hair grew from his cheeks and chin and his mouth was crooked. He was scrawny, besides, and by the look of things, hadn't made the acquaintance of water and soap in years.

2

"*You* have a wife?" Fargo said.

"I sure do. Her name is"—he paused for almost five seconds—"Clementine. And don't forget our five young'uns. There's, uh, Sally and Chester and, uh, Penelope, and, uh, the other two."

"As a liar, you're downright pitiful."

"What makes you think I ain't tellin' the truth?"

Fargo sniffed.

"Oh. Well, it could be my missus doesn't mind stink. Some females don't use their noses much."

"Do you ever listen to yourself?"

"What?"

"How about if I shoot you in the leg?" Fargo said. "Will you still claim you're married?"

"I'd get a divorce right quick."

Fargo smothered a grin. This assassin was about as intimidating as a kitten. "What's your handle?"

"Chester."

"You just said that's the name of your son."

"It's my name, too," Chester said. "It was all I could come up with. I thought of sayin' my son's name was Socks. That's what I call my horse on account of he has white on each leg down near his hoof. When I first got him I was goin' to call him Floyd after my pa but then I figured Socks was fancier."

Fargo stared.

"What?" Chester said.

"Who sent you to kill me?"

"I'd rather not say."

Fargo raised the Colt. "Stretch your leg out so I can be sure to hit your knee. When you're done rolling around, we'll talk some more."

"Hold on!" Chester bleated. "I'll tell you! I'll tell you!"

"Before Christmas," Fargo said.

"That ain't for months yet. It's only summer. You must have your months mixed up. The way to remember is that in the summer it's hot, and Christmas is when it's cold. That's how I remember it."

"Chester?"

"Yes, sir?"

"Who the hell hired you?"

"You won't believe me. I wouldn't believe me and I was there. I thought maybe I was seein' things since I was drunk at the time. But Hardy and Wilson saw whoever they were, too, so it wasn't like that time I drank so much bug juice, I saw a little green feller with pointy shoes dancin' in the middle of the street."

"Are you doing this on purpose?"

"Doin' what?"

"Get back to who hired you. What're their names and where do I find them?"

"It was just one. I guess you could call him the Hood, which ain't much of a name. I guess you could call him Shiny Boots since his were but I wasn't lookin' at his boots much with him in that hood."

Fargo took a step back and studied him.

"What?" Chester said again.

"The man who hired you wore a hood?"

"Ain't that what I just told you? He met us out back of the saloon and that's what he was wearin'. Although now that I think about it, it might have been a burlap sack. So maybe we should call him the Sack."

"And he hired *you* to kill me?"

"Well, it was Hardy the feller got word to." Chester nodded at the first man Fargo had shot. "That's Hardy, there. He was as bad as they come. He'd killed five or six folks. I can't remember which. And there was nothin' he liked more than robbin' and stealin'." He nodded at the other body. "Wilson, there, was a badman, too. But he liked puppies so I reckon he wasn't as bad as Hardy."

"How did you end up with two hard cases?"

"I sort of begged," Chester said. "I told them how I'd always wanted to be a badman. And how I'd cook for them and take care of their horses and do anything if they'd teach me how to be bad like they were. They laughed and slapped me around some, and finally Hardy said it might be fun to have me around, sort of like a pet was how he put it."

"Your dream in life is to be an outlaw?"

"Not that so much as to have folks be scared of me. Ever since I was little, people have picked on me because I'm, well, ugly. You know what it's like to be teased all the time? Probably not, a handsome galoot like you. But me, I look in a mirror and the glass cracks."

"Chester?"

"Sir?"

"The Hood. Or the Sack."

"Oh. Well, like I said, he got word to Hardy, and we went and met out back of the saloon, and this Hood or Sack told Hardy we'd get a thousand dollars if we put windows in your noggin."

Fargo was genuinely shocked. A thousand dollars was a lot of

4

money. Who did he know with that much to throw around who might want him dead? "Did you recognize the voice?"

Chester shook his head. "It was muffled by the sack. And, too, I got the idea the feller wasn't talkin' as he normally would. It was sort of like he had rocks in his mouth, or maybe cotton, since rocks are hard and can hurt."

"How did you know where to find me?"

"The Sack said as how you were headin' for Lodestone, and if we kept watch along the road from Denver, sooner or later we'd spot a gent on a pinto and it would be you. Sure enough, just before the sun went down, we spotted you comin' up the mountain and Hardy said we'd wait until you were asleep and do you in. Only you weren't asleep—you were playin' possum. And now he's dead and Wilson's dead and I have no one to teach me how to make folks be scared of me."

Fargo was curious. "Have you ever killed anyone?"

"Me? I ain't ever even beat anyone up. This would have been my first time, but between you and me, I wasn't sure I could go through with it. My stomach was flippin' up and down the whole time we snuck up on you. I figured I'd let Hardy and Wilson do the shootin' and I'd pretend I did."

"How would you pretend to kill me?"

"By pointin' my pistol at the ground and shootin' the dirt. It don't hurt anybody when you shoot dirt."

"Just when you think you've heard it all," Fargo said.

"I ain't hardly started," Chester said. "Do you want to hear about the time my pa whaled on me with a switch because I used his razor to shave the dog? He about took all my skin off, he was so mad. Drug me out of the house by the scruff of my neck and . . ."

Fargo held up his other hand.

"You don't want to hear my story?"

"Not this side of hell, no."

"Well, that's rude."

"What's your last name?"

"Leghorny."

"Your real last name."

"As God is my witness," Chester said. "I didn't like it much growin' up. It wasn't bad enough bein' teased about how I look. I got teased about my name a lot, too. I wanted to change it but Pa said if it was good enough for him and his pa, then it was good enough for me and if I changed it he'd take his switch to me. He was awful fond

5

of usin' that thing and I didn't want to give him an excuse so I kept my name Leghorny and here I am."

Fargo had a sense he had learned all he was going to, and then some, about the man who'd hired the assassins. But he tried anyway. "Did the Sack say why he wants me dead?"

"He might have told Hardy, but he didn't tell me. Fact is, when we met him out back of the saloon, he looked at me with those eyes-in-a-sack and asked what I was doin' there. Wilson stood up for me and said I was part of the deal and take it or leave it and the Sack took it."

Fargo had a lot to ponder but first things first. "Drag your friends off into the trees yonder."

Chester stepped to Hardy and bent and gripped his wrists, then looked up. "You're not goin' to help?"

"Drag," Fargo said.

Grumbling, Chester Leghorny hauled both badmen into the woods. He was still grumbling when Fargo marched him at gunpoint to the fire and made him sit with his hands behind his back.

"You're fixin' to tie me? Why not let me go?"

"I'm turning you over to the law in Lodestone," Fargo revealed.

"What for?" Chester asked, incredulous.

"For hiring out to kill me."

"But I didn't go through with it. It's not against the law to say you'll do somethin'. It's only against the law when you do it."

"I'm turning you over to the law anyway."

"Well, hell," Chester said. "What's this country comin' to when a man doesn't do somethin' and he still gets thrown in jail? You've ruined my day. I could use a drink right about now."

"Makes two of us," Fargo said.

2

Lodestone had sprung up barely a year and a half ago. A prospector had found some color in a creek and traced it to a vein. He filed a claim, then made the mistake of going to Denver to treat himself to a painted lady and crowed about how rich he was going to be. He downed so much booze, it took him three days to recover. When he finally made it back into the mountains, he discovered a tent city had sprung up.

Lodestone was born.

Like other boomtowns, it thrived. The gold practically jumped out of the ground. Log and frame buildings replaced the tents. Bustling saloons and businesses lined the streets.

Or so Fargo had heard. But now, as he wound down the last stretch of road leading Chester's horse and the two that belonged to Hardy and Wilson, he saw streets that were almost empty. Instead of the hubbub of voices, he heard only the bark of a dog.

Chester Leghorny noticed, too. "Why, look at that. There's hardly anybody around. How can that be?"

"You don't know?"

"How would I? I've never been to Lodestone before."

"Isn't that where the man who wore the sack hired you?"

Chester shook his head. "It was over to Silver Creek. Didn't I mention that? If I didn't, it was because I was flustered, what with you killin' my pards and all."

Fargo's puzzlement grew. He knew no one in Silver Creek. He'd never even been there. As best he recollected, it came into being a couple of years ago, thanks to a silver strike, and was about fifty miles from Lodestone, over the Divide.

"I wanted to stop here on the way to find you, but Hardy refused," Chester was saying. "He said the job came first. That after we killed you, we could spend a couple of days in Lodestone." Chester sighed. "So much for havin' fun."

"Maybe the marshal will let you have a night on the town before he throws you behind bars."

Chester brightened. "Do you really reckon he would? Not that I could have much of a night, me bein' broke and all." He paused. "Wait. You were joshin', weren't you?"

"What do you think?"

"I don't, mostly. It tires my brain too much. The best way to go through life is not to think at all."

"You seem to have the hang of it."

"Why, thank you. I've tried hard not to let my brain get in the way of me havin' a good time."

They reached the end of the main street. Some of the businesses were boarded over and many of the homes had an air of neglect.

The marshal's office was smack in the middle of town.

Fargo dismounted at the hitch rail, stepped to the door, and worked the latch. The door wouldn't open. He stepped to the dusty window and peered in. No one was there. Figuring the lawman was off on his rounds, he leaned against the overhang post and said, "We'll wait a spell."

"Mind helpin' me down? Folks are starin'."

"You're not helpless."

"But my hands are tied. How am I supposed to climb off without hands?"

"Use your head."

"That won't do any good. I can't take hold of the saddle horn with my ear, now, can I?"

Fargo walked around the rail. Reaching up, he grabbed Chester by the shirt and pulled.

Chester squawked as he left the saddle. He landed on his side, and puffs of dust rose. Coughing and swearing, he rose onto an elbow and glared. "That wasn't very nice."

"You wanted off."

A pair of townsmen bustled up. One was heavyset with wide side-whiskers and wore a bowler. The other was skinny and favored a derby. Both wore waistcoats and had diamond stickpins in their cravats.

The one with the whiskers asked, "What's going on here?"

"I'm bein' abused," Chester said. "There I was, mindin' my own business at my campfire, when this hombre popped out of nowhere and conked me over the head and . . ."

With a flick of his wrist, Fargo had the Colt out. He pressed the muzzle to Chester's temple.

"Here now," said the skinny man in the derby. "We'll have none of that."

"Not one more word," Fargo said to Chester.

"Nary any?"

"That was two." Fargo thumbed back the hammer.

Chester blanched and opened his mouth but closed it again and gave a slight shake of his head.

Fargo faced the townsmen. "This gent and two others were hired to kill me. I want him behind bars."

"Hold on," said the man with whiskers. "Why should we believe you and not him? Who are you, anyhow, to wave guns at people?"

Fargo told them.

The townsmen looked at each other, and the man with whiskers grinned and thrust out a hand. "Why, you're the very one we sent for. I'm Mayor Quilby, by the way, and this is Arthur Thomas, the town treasurer."

"Quilby?" Fargo repeated, and fished a folded envelope from his pocket. "It was you who wrote me."

"Indeed, I did," Mayor Quilby said. He seemed to remember that Chester was there. "You say this shifty-looking person tried to kill you?"

"How come you'll take his word and not mine?" Chester demanded. "Who is he, anyhow, that you sent for him?"

It was Arthur Thomas who answered. "Mr. Fargo, for your information, is considered one of the best scouts alive, if not *the* best. The army calls on his services all the time, and he's guided wagon trains and whatnot on occasion. Or so the newspapers say."

Mayor Quilby threw in, "He also has a reputation for being a man of his word. Which is why we'll believe him before we'll believe someone like you."

"Like me how?" Chester said. "Because I'm ugly as sin?"

"You do look like a weasel," Arthur Thomas said.

"It's those shifty eyes," Mayor Quilby said. "They're never still."

"It's a fine how-do-you-do when ugly gets a man thrown in jail," Chester said indignantly.

"About that," Mayor Quilby said, and turned to Fargo. "I'm afraid if you want him behind bars, you'll have to put him there yourself."

"Where's your marshal?"

"We don't have one," Arthur Thomas replied. "He quit on account of we couldn't afford to pay him."

"Not with the town going bust," the mayor said. "I had to cut my own pay by half, if you can believe it."

"Your letter said something about five hundred dollars," Fargo reminded them. "How do you aim to pay me?"

"Don't worry in that regard," Mayor Quilby said. "The town council set aside the funds. I'll call a meeting in, say, twenty minutes, and we'll explain why we sent for you. How would that be?"

"It wouldn't," Fargo said. "I want to wash up and have something to eat and a drink or three. Make it two hours."

"That long?" Arthur Thomas said.

"Now, now," Mayor Quilby said. "Mr. Fargo has ridden a long way to get here. He must be tired and hungry."

"It's just that so much depends on this," Arthur Thomas said. "The longer we wait, the more time it gives them."

"Gives who?" Fargo asked.

"We'll discuss all that at the meeting. In the meantime . . ." The mayor fished in a pocket and produced a ring of keys. He jangled them, then went from one to the next, saying to himself, "Is this it? Is this it? Is this it?" Finally he let out an "Ah. Here's the one to the marshal's office." He walked over, unlocked the door, and pushed. The door creaked open, spilling dust motes into the air.

"I'd just as soon you didn't lock me up," Chester Leghorny said. "How about if I give you my word I'll behave and treat you to a drink?"

Taking hold of his arm, Fargo shoved Chester at the doorway. "Inside." In his estimation, the would-be tough man had no more gumption than a puppy. But a thousand dollars might make Chester rustle some up, and he didn't want to be looking over his shoulder every minute.

"You have a lot of bark on you," Chester complained.

The marshal had been a tidy cuss. Papers were neatly stacked on the desk, and everything was in its place.

"It's a shame Marshal Hadrock refused to stay on," Mayor Quilby remarked. "We assured him that he would receive his pay as soon as we were back on our financial feet, but he left anyway."

"A real shame," the treasurer echoed.

The single cell had a bunk that had been made up. Fargo took Chester over, untied him, and gave him a light push.

Chester stumbled and shammed nearly falling to his knees. "Did you see what he did to me?" he said to the townsmen. "There's no need to be so rough, is there?"

"You are a faker, sir," Mayor Quilby said. "I saw with my own eyes that he barely touched you."

"You need spectacles," Chester said.

Fargo slammed the door, and at the clang, Chester jumped. "I'll check in on you later."

Chester came to the bars. "You're goin' to leave me here all by my lonesome? There's nothin' to do. I'll die of boredom."

"One can only hope," Fargo said. He hung the key on a peg and went out with His Honor and the treasurer at his heels. About a dozen people had gathered and were watching with interest. One of them, a huge woman in a green bonnet and dress, wagged a pudgy finger.

"Is this him, Mayor? The one we sent for?"

"The very one, Gladiola," Mayor Quilby said. "We're holding a town meeting in two hours, and I expect you to be there."

"Don't worry on that score." Gladiola came up to Fargo and raked him from head to toe with eyes that made him think of a ferret's. "I hope you're all it's claimed you are, mister."

"Ma'am?" Fargo said.

"Are you hard of hearing?" Gladiola said. "You'd better be as good as everyone says. If you don't get us there, I will take it personal and by-God trounce you."

"Ma'am?" Fargo said again. "Did you just threaten me?"

Gladiola shook a fist in his face. "I'll do more than threaten. Ask anyone. I've whipped men bigger than you." She tapped him on the jaw with her knuckles.

Fargo's temper flared. "Now listen, lady . . ." he began.

"Here now," Mayor Quilby said, stepping between them and putting his hands on Gladiola's shoulders. "Is that any way to greet him? We haven't even told him what we want yet."

"He needs to understand," Gladiola declared. "I don't suffer incompetents." She wheeled, and holding her handbag delicately in her left hand, swayed off like a schooner in a strong wind.

"Sorry about that," Quilby said to Fargo. "Miss Gladiola Thimblebottom is one of the town's leading citizens."

"Thimblebottom?" Fargo said, and snorted. First Leghorny, now this.

"Gladiola tends to overstep herself," Arthur Thomas said.

"Just tread easy around her like everyone else does," the mayor advised. "She wasn't joshing about beating the tar out of you."

Arthur Thomas said. "She will fight any man at the drop of a feather."

"And she'll drop the feather herself," Mayor Quilby said. He stared after the departing tent and gave a slight tremble.

"Are there any men in this town?" Fargo asked. He didn't wait for them to answer. Wheeling, he strode down the street to a saloon and shouldered through the batwings.

The place was dead. A scruffy bartender was dozing with his chin in his hand, and a fly buzzed at the front window.

Spurs jingling, Fargo went over and pounded the bar.

The barkeep jumped and looked around in confusion and then blurted, "My God. A customer."

"Monongahela," Fargo said. "And leave the bottle."

"Sure thing." Grinning happily, the bartender snatched a bottle from a shelf and eagerly filled a glass to the brim. "How do you do? I'm called Olives."

About to raise the glass, Fargo shook his head and said, "You have got to be joshing me."

"I beg your pardon?"

"What kind of name is Olives?"

"What's wrong with it? I like them more than anything. It beats being called Outhouse or Horse Poop."

Fargo polished off the glass at a gulp.

"Lord Almighty, mister," Olives said. "You take your drinking serious."

Fargo refilled the glass, chugged, and smacked the empty glass down.

"I wish I could drink like you," Olives said. "But if I have half a glass, I'm tipsy. The only one I know who can hold a candle to you is her."

"Her who?" Fargo asked while pouring.

Olives nodded toward the back of the saloon.

Fargo turned and whistled. "Well, now," he said.

Lodestone had just become a whole lot more interesting.

3

She wore a red dress cut low to show off her ample cleavage. As she sashayed toward the bar, the dress clung to her willowy thighs, leaving little to the imagination. Her hair was as red as the dress, her lips full rubies, her dancing eyes as blue as a mountain lake. Her nails were painted, and she had rouge on her cheeks and had done something to her long eyelashes so that they curled upward. She came to a stop and looked Fargo up and down and said in a husky voice, "My, oh my. What do we have here?"

"He just showed up," Olives said. "I ain't had a chance to holler for you yet."

"When someone as handsome as this galoot strolls in, you holler right away." The redhead placed her hand on her hips and posed seductively. "You sure are easy on the eyes, mister."

"Works both ways," Fargo said. He supposed he shouldn't be surprised to find a dove of quality. Not that long ago, Lodestone had been a top-class proposition.

"Any objections to buying a girl a drink?"

"A glass for the lady," Fargo said.

Olives scrambled to produce one.

The redhead leaned her elbow on the counter and rimmed her lips with the tip of her tongue. "I hope you plan to stick around a while."

"I'm to meet with the mayor in a couple of hours," Fargo said. "Plenty of time for us to become acquainted."

"Quilby?" The redhead blinked. "Say, you must be the gent he sent for. The one he said would lead us to our new home."

"Your what?"

"I'll let him explain." She smiled and touched his cheek. "We have other things to occupy us. What's your handle, anyhow?"

"For you, I answer to Skye."

"Most hereabouts call me Horace."

About to fill her glass, Fargo said, "Horace? I must not have heard right."

"You did."

"This is some town."

"My real name is Hortense, but I've never liked it much. One day some of the gents were joshing me and said as how I should call myself Horace instead. Pretty soon everybody was calling me that."

"I'll stick with Hortense," Fargo said.

"I sort of like Horace myself," Olives interjected. "It's funny, her having a gent's name."

"Just as funny as you having a gal's name," Fargo said.

"Olives ain't female. Everybody eats olives."

"Why are you standing there?"

"Eh?"

"Don't you have something to do?"

Olives grew red in the face. He went to say something, thought better of it, and moved off muttering.

"You shouldn't ought to be mean to him," Hortense said. "He's a nice guy."

Eyeing her hungrily, Fargo said, "So are you."

Hortense laughed. "I knew we'd hit it off. How about if we mosey over to my room? I have cookies if you're hungry. I like to treat my customers to a little extra so they'll come back for more."

Fargo admired the sweep of her bosom and imagined holding her jugs in his hands. "Who needs cookies with tits as big as yours?"

This time Hortense cackled. "What a sweet thing to say." She hooked her arm in his. "Bring the bottle and we'll be on our way."

Fargo remembered to slap down a coin to pay for the Mononga- hela. He didn't ask for change, although he had some coming. He thought that would mollify Olives, but the barkeep frowned at him as he walked out.

No sooner had the batwings swung behind them than Fargo had to draw up short to keep from colliding with someone about to enter. The newcomer was as tall as he was and outweighed him by a good forty pounds. Dressed in ill-fitting store-bought clothes that were speckled with bits of straw and brown smudges, the man smelled of horse manure.

"Horace!" he exclaimed. "I was coming to see you." He pulled a poke from his pocket and jiggled it. "I've got the money for another turn."

Hortense smiled and patted his arm. "I'm afraid I'm busy at the moment, Mouse. Come back later."

"Mouse?" Fargo said.

"What's the matter with my name?" the slab of muscle asked. "I've been called that since I was little."

"You're not little now," Fargo said. "A better name would be Moose."

"What's a 'moose'?"

"Mouse," Hortense said to Fargo, "runs the stable. He pays me a visit every chance he gets."

"What's a 'moose'?" Mouse asked again.

"They're like an elk," Fargo explained, "only with a bigger nose and different antlers."

Mouse put a hand to his face. "What's wrong with my nose?"

"Nothing."

"You just said I'm a moose and then you said moose have big noses. That must mean you think I have a big nose. I sure don't have antlers."

"This is some town," Fargo said again.

"Calm down, Mouse," Hortense said. "He didn't mean anything. Skye, here, is the gentleman the mayor sent for."

"I don't care," Mouse said. "I don't like people poking fun at me."

"All I was saying," Fargo tried again, "is that you're awful big to be named after a damn rodent."

"What's a 'rodent'?"

"Oh, hell," Fargo said.

"Tell me what a rodent is."

"Rats and such," Fargo said.

"Now I'm a rat?"

"Mouse, please," Hortense said. "You're making a mountain out of a molehill. He doesn't mean anything by it."

"First he calls me a moose, and then he calls me a rat. If that's not poking fun I don't know what is."

"There's one thing I haven't called you yet," Fargo said.

"What would that be?"

Fargo knew better. He knew that if he said what he was about to say, there would be hell to pay. But he'd reached the limits of his patience. "A jackass."

"Oh, no," Hortense said, and took a quick step back.

Mouse turned as red as her hair, and his jaw twitched. "I knew it. I knew you were poking fun." He stuffed the poke in his pocket.

"You might want to put down that bottle unless you're fixing to conk me over the head with it."

Fargo handed the Monongahela to Hortense.

"Mayor Quilby won't like this," she appealed to the stableman. "This man is to be our guide, remember?"

"I won't break anything," Mouse said. "All I'll do is learn him not to go around calling folks Moose."

"When they passed out brains," Fargo said, "where were you?"

Mouse rumbled deep in his wide chest. Flinging his arms wide, he drove at Fargo like a mad bull. Fargo tried to sidestep, but Mouse rammed him off his feet and smashed him against the wall. He felt the air whoosh out of his lungs even as Mouse drove a fist into his gut.

Fargo nearly blacked out. Slipping clear, he flicked a right cross that did little more than make Mouse blink. He arched his knee up and in, but all Mouse did was grunt.

"That was dirty."

Fargo whipped a hook that caught Mouse on the jaw. It was like hitting a blacksmith's anvil. Mouse dived at Fargo's legs, but Fargo bounded to one side. Mouse immediately spun and dived again.

Iron clamps wrapped around Fargo's shins, and he crashed onto his back. The world spun, and his ears rang, and Mouse straddled him.

"Got you now."

Fargo's vision cleared just as a fist drove at his face. He twisted, and Mouse struck the ground instead.

"Ow!"

Fargo planted a fist in Mouse's gut but Mouse didn't even blink. Hortense was hollering something.

Mouse ignored her. He gripped Fargo's jaw to hold Fargo's head still, and cocked his other fist.

"Going to bust your teeth!"

Fargo sank those teeth into Mouse's thumb. Mouse yelped and jerked his arm back, and Fargo punched him in the neck. Crying out, Mouse rose and backed off a couple of steps.

"Please stop!" Hortense cried.

"He hurt me," Mouse said, and waded in again.

Fargo was up and ready. He avoided a grab at his left arm and connected with his right fist to Mouse's ribs. He might as well have hit metal bars. Mouse growled and backhanded him, sending him tottering. He recovered as Mouse sprang. Quick as thought, he landed two solid punches that jolted Mouse onto his heels. Undaunted, Mouse threw himself at Fargo's feet, seeking to upend him like before. Fargo kicked and spun and was in the clear.

"Damn, you're quick," Mouse complained.

Fargo raised both fists.

Suddenly Mayor Quilby was there, pushing on Mouse's chest. "Enough, Mouse! Enough, I say!"

Fargo's estimation of Quilby rose a notch. It took grit to stand up to someone that size.

"He called me a moose!" Mouse said, attempting to push the mayor aside. "Get out of the way."

"You will cease and desist—do you hear me?" Quilby held his ground. "This gentleman is here at my express invitation, and I won't have you harm him."

"Didn't you hear me? He called me a moose, damn it."

"So?" Quilby said. "Moose are fine animals."

"They are?"

Mayor Quilby nodded. "Certainly. Why, up in Canada, the people there revere the moose. They say it's a noble animal, and often name their children after it."

"They do?"

"Would I lie to you?" Quilby said. "I'm the mayor, aren't I?"

"Yes," Mouse said, nodding, "and you know a lot of stuff."

"This man actually paid you a compliment."

"He called me a rat, too," Mouse said.

"Can you blame him? He praised you, and what did you do?"

Some of the wind went out of Mouse's anger. Deflating, he said contritely, "I got mad."

"You do that much too often," Quilby said. "The last time it was the drummer you thought slighted you when he wanted to sell you tweezers."

"He said my nose was hairy," Mouse said.

"My point," Mayor Quilby said, "is that you can't go around stomping people over assumed insults. Didn't we agree that you would come ask me if something is an insult or not?"

"We did," Mouse said sullenly.

"And now that I've explained about the moose, what do you say to Mr. Fargo, here?"

Mouse hung his head in shame. "Sorry, mister. I ain't ever been called a moose before. Thank you for calling me one."

Fargo was almost too dumbfounded to say, "That's all right."

Mouse impulsively held out a hand to shake. "No hard feelings? You can call me a moose all you want from now on."

Fargo shook.

Turning to go, Mouse said to Hortense, "I'll be back later for that poke. About six or so. Would that be all right?"

"Perfectly fine," Hortense said sweetly.

Mouse nodded and lumbered off.

The mayor waited until the stableman was out of earshot to say, "I almost felt bad about that. But he really must learn to control his temper." He turned and clapped Fargo on the arm. "All's well that ends well, I always say. You'll still attend the town council meeting and hear us out?"

"I came this far," Fargo said.

"Understood." Quilby smiled at Hortense. "As for you, young lady, I'd like you to treat Mr. Fargo on the house, as it were."

"Let him poke me for free?" Hortense said in amazement.

"Just this once. To show our appreciation."

"Let him poke your wife, then," Hortense said.

"No need to be crude," Quilby said. "Married women don't poke other men. Besides, Augustina has a limit of one poke a month, and I already gave her the poke for this month."

"Once a month?" Fargo said.

"It used to be twice, but she lost interest once she turned forty. She says that's common with females. Pokes aren't as important to them as they are to men."

"They are to me," Hortense said, "and I never do it for free."

"Very well," Mayor Quilby said. "There's enough in petty cash, I believe. If Arthur wants to know what it's for, I'll have him write in the ledger that we used it for civic relations." He smiled and touched the brim of his bowler and walked off humming to himself.

"I've said it before and I'll say it again," Fargo said. "This some town."

4

Fargo figured that Hortense had a room at a boardinghouse but she had a suite on the top floor of Lodestone's grandest hotel. Typical of boomtowns, every room oozed luxury: polished hardwood floors with carpets and tapestries, mahogany furniture, glass cabinets, expensive curtains over the windows. "Do you have your own gold mine?" he joked.

Hortense had set out large crystal glasses and was filling them from his whiskey bottle. "As a matter of fact, I do." Grinning, she cupped her breasts, then ran a hand lower. "Three of them."

Fargo laughed.

A wistful look came over her. "For a while there I was making more money than a banker. There was so much floating around the town, it was scary. I charged ten times what I'd ask in places like Denver or Saint Louis." She stopped, then sadly concluded, "But now all the gold has dried up."

"That's why Lodestone is turning into a ghost town."

Hortense nodded. "I hate it. I like living in luxury."

Fargo never had cared all that much about the so-called finer things in life. Give him a campfire and some venison or buffalo meat and a clear night sparkling with stars and he was content.

"A lot of us had it good," Hortense related. "With Lodestone going bust, we've had to take drastic steps so we can have it good again."

"Such as?" Fargo asked.

Hortense put the bottle down. "Why are we talking business? The mayor will tell you about it at the council meeting." She handed him a glass and raised hers. "To hot and delicious sex," she proposed with a grin.

Fargo clinked his glass to hers and drank. They were seated on a settee with cushions so soft, it was like settling into a bed. "I can see how someone could get used to this."

"More than used to," Hortense said, gazing about. "After years of struggling, it is wonderful to have everything I've ever dreamed of having."

Fargo shrugged. "Find another boomtown."

Hortense smiled. "Our thinking exactly." She set her glass down and slid so close, her leg brushed his. "Didn't you say you only have a couple of hours to kill?"

Fargo inhaled the fragrance of her perfume and felt the warmth of her body through her dress. "About an hour and a half by now."

"Then why are we wasting time talking about things we can talk about later when I'd much rather see you naked?"

"A woman after my own heart." Fargo reached past her to put his own glass on the same small table, and their mouths met in a velvet kiss. Her lips parted, her tongue entwining with his.

Hortense wriggled and cooed and squirmed her bottom.

Fargo felt a familiar need, the craving that wouldn't be denied. It had surprised him greatly when he was younger to learn that not all men felt the same. Some, in fact, saw making love as a bother. Some women, too, like the mayor's wife. Him, he couldn't go without for long or an urge came over him that eclipsed all else. He cupped a breast and squeezed and felt it swell under his hand.

"Nice," Hortense said huskily, as they broke for breath. "How about we go where we can be more comfortable?"

"The street?"

Hortense chortled. "Wouldn't that be a spectacle? Everyone left in town would come to watch. But no. I was thinking my bedroom."

"Lead the way."

In the middle was a four-poster with a canopy, custom-made, Hortense told him, which explained why it was twice the size of any four-poster he'd ever seen. The canopy and quilt and pillowcases were red, like her dress.

"The color I like when I'm doing it," she told him.

Fargo hadn't ever heard of anyone having a favorite color for *that*. But then, people had a lot of odd quirks.

Scooping Hortense up, Fargo laid her on the bed and stretched out beside her. Kissing and caressing, they melted into each other, while divesting themselves of their clothes. Presently they were naked, and Fargo leaned back to admire her.

Hortense wasn't out in the sun much. Her skin had an alabaster cast, which resembled the china in her cabinet. Her neck was flawlessly smooth, her breasts firm, the tips upswept, so that her long nipples jutted invitingly. Her stomach was as flat as his but smooth where his was knotted with muscle. Below was the perfect triangle of her thatch. Her thighs were as soft as the settee cushions. Small feet with red toenails capped the exquisite portrait she presented.

"Like what you see, big man?" Hortense teased.

"Do you really need to ask?" Fargo bent to a nipple. Inhaling it, he tweaked it with his tongue and lathered the aureole. She moaned and placed a hand in his hair and crooked a knee so that it rubbed his manhood.

Fargo's hunger climbed. He switched to her other breast while his hands sculpted and kneaded everywhere he could reach.

Hortense did the same, and then some. There was a reason she had risen to the top of her profession. She knew things to do many women didn't. Little tricks, such as sensitive spots that drove a man crazy. With her tongue and her fingers she was akin to a maestro on a piano, playing a man's body to the tune of her passion.

Making love to her was an experience.

Fargo lost himself in sensation. He had no sense of time, of anything other than this beautiful creature who seemed to read his mind when it came to doing all the things he liked to do.

He'd known a lot of women in his travels but few rivaled Hortense. She was in a carnal class by herself.

Their mutual explosion shook the four-poster bed. The canopy quaked so violently, it was a wonder it didn't crash down on top of them.

Afterward, Fargo lay glistening with sweat and collecting his breath as Hortense rolled onto her back and closed her eyes and smiled.

"Damnation," Hortense exclaimed.

"What?"

"You are one of the best, ever."

"I thank you, ma'am. The feeling's mutual."

"I'm serious."

"So am I."

Hortense cracked an eye and squinted at him. "I'm glad Quilby sent for you. I just hope everything goes well."

"We're back to business talk already?"

Hortense grinned and stretched like a cat. "Can I ask something of you?"

"Pretty much anything."

"Don't hold it against me if it all goes to hell. Everyone took part in the vote so don't just blame me."

"What are you talking about?"

Hortense looked at a clock. "You'll find out in about twenty minutes. I'd better get up and put myself together." She rolled toward him and playfully kissed him on the nose. "If you ever want a second helping, I'm more than willing."

"How about after the council meeting?"

"You might have other things on your mind by then," Hortense said enigmatically. She kissed him again and scooted off the bed. "Twenty minutes," she repeated, and moved toward a doorway.

Fargo wasn't in any hurry. It'd only take him a minute to dress and strap his Colt around his waist. He closed his eyes and lay there fully relaxed, a rare state for him.

When he heard a door creak he looked over, thinking Hortense had come back in and he'd catch a last sight of her naked. But it was the other door, the door to the parlor.

A man was standing there, and he was raising a rifle to his shoulder.

Fargo half thought he must have been imagining things. Then he heard the click of the hammer.

Exploding off the bed as the rifle thundered, Fargo dived onto the floor next to his clothes and his holster. As he grabbed the Colt, boots drummed. He looked up just as the assassin came around the end of the bed. The man fired but rushed his shot and missed. Fargo squeezed the trigger and the shooter staggered. He squeezed off another and the man buckled. In a bound, Fargo kicked the rifle from his grasp.

Hortense came running, a towel around her. "What on earth?"

Fargo studied his attacker, a lanky hombre wearing cheap store-bought clothes and scuffed boots. The man was gulping for breath. "Why?" Fargo said.

The man's eyes narrowed.

"Who the hell are you? Why'd you try to buck me out in gore?"

The man tried to speak but all that came out of his mouth was scarlet rivulets.

He coughed and quaked.

Hortense had reached them. "Dear God," she said, putting a hand to her throat. "He tried to kill you?"

Fargo nodded. "Do you know him? Is he one of your customers?"

"I never saw him before in my life."

Fargo sank to a knee and shook the man's chin. "Don't die on me yet. Tell me why, damn you."

The man seemed to make a mighty effort and gasped, "Can't let them—" He stopped and arched his back, and died.

"Hell," Fargo said.

"You were lucky he didn't kill you."

"Damn lucky," Fargo agreed. Setting the Colt down, he went through the man's pockets. All he found were lucifers and several coins. He noticed that the man's hat had partly fallen off and spied something inside it, tucked under the band. Pulling the hat off, he turned it over. "What do you know?"

"You found something?"

Fargo held up a wad of bills. "I'd call this something." He counted them. "Five hundred dollars."

"What could he be doing with so much?"

"My guess," Fargo said, "is that it's what he was paid to kill me."

"Someone wants you dead?"

Fargo hadn't told her about the attempt on the trail. Now he did, ending with "I've got Chester over to the jail."

"So this makes twice," Hortense said. "It sounds serious."

"No fooling. Go get dressed."

"Why do you sound so mad?"

Fargo looked at her.

"Oh." Hortense hurried away.

Sitting on the edge of the bed, Fargo thoughtfully regarded the body. From here on out, he didn't dare let down his guard. Whoever was out to bury him evidently had a lot of money to throw around. A thousand for the first three and now five hundred for this one. The man in the sack could afford to keep at it until someone succeeded.

"'Can't let them'?" Fargo repeated the man's dying words. Can't let *who*? "Them" meant more than one.

Rousing, he hurriedly dressed. He replaced the spent cartridges, twirled the Colt into his holster, and went out to the parlor. The front door was open. He couldn't recollect if Hortense had thrown the bolt when they got there but he didn't think she had. They'd been too busy groping each other.

He sat drinking and mulling things over until Hortense swirled out of the bedroom in a different red dress. She was smiling but her smile faded when she saw his expression.

"Sort of spoiled the mood, didn't it?" she said.

Fargo polished off the glass.

"Do you have any idea why anyone would want to kill you?"

"I'm told I cuss a lot."

Hortense laughed. "That's good. I always say there's nothing in life so terrible that we can't make light of it."

"I make light of grizzlies and Apaches all the time," Fargo said.

"Now you're mocking me."

Fargo stood and held out his arm and she took it. "How many people are left in Lodestone?"

"Oh, about thirty or so. Why do you ask?"

"Just wondered."

"You'll see them at the meeting. Everyone will be there. Olives is closing the saloon and the other business owners will do the same. The town will be next to dead."

"It already is."

"I know," Hortense said, and her sad look returned.

Fargo was careful to scan the street as they emerged. The next assassin might be smarter and attempt to pick him off from a distance. He walked with his right hand on his Colt.

"I can't wait for you to hear the mayor's proposal." Hortense perked up. "We have a lot riding on your answer."

"What can I do that's so important?"

"The mayor will explain," Hortense said. "You don't know it yet, but you're the answer to our prayers."

"I've been a lot of things but never that."

"Look around you," Hortense said, gesturing at the empty buildings. "We're dying here. Without your help, in a month or two we'll all have to head elsewhere. Scoff if you must, but yes, some of us have prayed for deliverance, and the Good Lord sent us you."

"I'll be damned," Fargo said.

5

Fargo had wondered why no one came to investigate the gunshots. Now he knew. Everyone was already at the meeting. When he entered with Hortense on his arm, the hubbub of talk ceased.

Lodestone's residents were seated on long benches. At the front of the room, on a raised platform, sat Mayor Quilby and Arthur Thomas, the town treasurer, and two others. A chair had been set near it, facing the benches.

"Ah, Mr. Fargo!" the mayor happily exclaimed on seeing him. "We've been eagerly awaiting your arrival." He motioned at the chair. "Have a seat, if you would, and we'll get under way."

Hortense let go of Fargo's arm and moved to a bench. Two men practically fell over themselves to make room.

Fargo sat and folded his arms across his chest. He wasn't used to being the center of so much attention. Everyone was staring. The looks they were giving him were unusual. It wasn't just curiosity. There was something more, something he couldn't quite peg.

Mayor Quilby cleared his throat. "Ladies and gentlemen, friends one and all, I welcome you to what may be our last town meeting."

Fargo noticed there weren't any children. Half a dozen couples but no families. He didn't think that strange. Boomtowns were too wild and woolly for those who wanted a settled, peaceful life with schools and churches and whatnot.

"All of you know why we're here," the mayor weny on. "Lodestone is dying. Our gold has played out and our beloved Lodestone is on the verge of becoming a ghost town."

"Damn our luck, anyhow," a man said angrily, and there were nods and murmurs of agreement.

"I've heard it said that the wise make their own luck," Mayor Quilby responded. "Yes, Lodestone is withering away. And, no, we can't prevent it. But that doesn't mean we have to give up and scatter to the four winds. We've had a good thing here. So why not have a good thing elsewhere?"

Fargo glanced over, wondering what Quilby was getting at.

"Most of our fellow Lodestoneites have already left. Those who didn't have any real investment in our prosperity. Those who go from boomtown to boomtown like dogs following a trail of bones. But not us. We want something better. We want something more permanent."

"You bet we do," someone declared.

"Which is why we've struck on the idea of staying together," Quilby said. "Of starting over. Of taking up where we've left off."

Fargo thought he savvied. They were fixing to start a new town. Find a site along, say, the Oregon Trail, and rebuild. It had been done before.

"We're all set to leave," Quilby continued. "Our wagons are packed and parked out back of the stable. All that remains is to retain the services of a guide." He looked at Fargo.

"Ah," Fargo said. He'd guided wagon trains on a few occasions. Mostly through hostile country where knowing the lay of the land was crucial. "So that's why you sent for me."

"It is, indeed," Mayor Quilby said. "We would like you to guide us to our new home."

"And where would that be?" Fargo imagined it must be far off. Perhaps toward the Green River country or the Great Salt Lake.

"Silver Creek," Mayor Quilby said.

Fargo grinned, thinking he was jesting. "Where is it really?"

"Silver Creek," the mayor said again.

Fargo sat up. "Silver Creek is just over the Divide."

"We know that," Quilby said.

"There's a road between here and there."

"We obviously know that, too."

"Then what in hell do you need me for? A blind man could find it with his head up his ass."

A woman gasped and whispers broke out.

"Now, now," Quilby addressed them. "We must bear with him. Mr. Fargo is rightfully annoyed. On the face of it, our wanting to hire him must seem preposterous."

"There's no 'seems' about it," Fargo said. "It's only fifty miles."

"It's not the distance. It's the security." Mayor Quilby paused. "I suppose you think we could hire just about anyone."

"You can get there yourselves," Fargo replied. It wasn't as if they'd need him to find water and shoot game. They could take enough water in their water barrels to last the trip, and game was plentiful.

"True," Mayor Quilby said. "Very true. But you see, there are other factors. The Utes, for instance."

"They've never attacked a wagon train that I know of."

"There's always a first time," Quilby said. "Plus it's well known that the mountains crawl with outlaws and ruffians of every stripe."

"You have enough men here that outlaws would think twice about tangling with you."

"Perhaps. But why not reduce the chance of that happening by hiring someone of your caliber?"

"It's only *fifty* miles," Fargo said again.

"I told you he'd think we were crazy," Arthur Thomas remarked.

Mayor Quilby regarded the people on the benches, then turned to Fargo. "Take a good look around you. These folks are store owners. Clerks. A seamstress. A baker. Hardly any of them have ever used a gun. None of them have ever killed a living soul."

"Yes, but . . ." Fargo began.

Quilby held up a hand. "Hear me out. You're aware of your reputation, are you not? I don't mean your fondness for liquor and cards or your dalliances with the ladies, either."

Nearly every head swung toward Hortense.

"I refer to your other reputation," Quilby said. "Folks say you're not someone to be trifled with. That you're as hard as nails. That you've shot more than your share of owlhoots and renegades and who-knows-else. That you've gone up against Apaches and Comanches and the Sioux and gotten the better of them. That you are, in short—and pardon my language, ladies—a deadly son of a bitch."

Fargo frowned. Yes, he'd been in more than a few shooting affrays and other scrapes where it was do or die, but the last thing he wanted was for it to get around that he was some sort of killer.

"Why do you look so upset?" Mayor Quilby asked. "The truth is the truth. You know how to take care of yourself. We, to be honest, don't. We're not fighters like you. I daresay, if some scoundrel came up to me and grabbed me by the front of my shirt and said he was going to thrash me, I'd plead with him not to. But if the same scoundrel were to do the same to you, you'd beat him senseless or shoot him. Am I right or am I right?"

"Well," Fargo said. But the mayor had a point; he never let anyone ride roughshod over him.

"There. You see? Is it any wonder we want to hire a man like you for even so short a trek? We'll feel completely safe with you as our wagon boss. So I ask you, on behalf of everyone here, if you'll agree to take us to Silver Creek."

Fargo saw that every last face was fixed on his expectantly.

Mayor Quilby wasn't done. "Five hundred dollars for fifty miles. Over a road, no less. Easy money, I should think, for a man like you."

The hell of it was, Fargo reflected, it would be. The trip shouldn't take more than two days.

"Yes or no?" Mayor Quilby asked. "We're on pins and needles here."

"Yes," Fargo said. He'd get it over with, take their money, and ride to Denver to treat himself to a high old time.

Whoops and clapping erupted.

The mayor joined in. When everyone was calm again he said, "You heard him, ladies and gentlemen. I hereby declare that we'll leave tomorrow at ten a.m. That should give all of you time to do whatever last-minute packing you have to do. I realize some of you will have to leave some of your possessions behind. The wagons can only hold so much. But take heart in the fact that in our new home, you can recover what you've lost. Or, for that matter, once we're there, you can send a wagon back for whatever you feel you can't live without."

The people of Lodestone were listening intently.

"What about when we get there?" Gladiola Thimblebottom asked. "You know what I mean."

"We've already talked that out, Gladiola," Quilby said curtly. "And now's not the time to bring it up again." He smiled and gestured. "For now, go home and finish preparing. Whoever isn't ready to depart on time will be left behind."

Fargo felt compelled to say, "I don't mind waiting a little longer to head out if I have to."

"That's courteous of you," Mayor Quilby said, "but we've been preparing for our exodus for weeks. It's important we reach Silver Creek without delay."

"If you say so," Fargo said.

"I do." Quilby turned to the good citizens of Lodestone. "Unless there's something else someone cares to bring up, I declare this meeting adjourned."

They began filing out. Several came to the front to personally thank Fargo. A few men shook his hand.

One of the last to step up to him was Hortense. "I'll be busy packing for a while, handsome, but if you'd like to stop by later, you're more than welcome."

"I believe I will," Fargo said. An entire night with her would be an experience to remember.

Then only the mayor was left, and he came over, too. "I want to thank you again for agreeing."

"I'd like the five hundred in advance."

"You don't trust us?" Quilby said with a lopsided grin.

"Just in case none of you make it there alive," Fargo joked.

Quilby laughed louder and longer than Fargo thought he should, then said, "I'll have the money for you in the morning, if that's all right."

"Fine," Fargo said. He also had the five hundred he'd taken from the man who'd tried to kill him at Hortense's, plus about fifty dollars of his own. "Do you reckon there's any chance of finding a card game to sit in on?"

"I very much doubt it. The professional gamblers have all left. The people who are left rarely indulge."

"Figures," Fargo said.

Quilby made to leave but stopped. "By the way, before I forget, what will you do with your own baggage, as it were?"

"All I have is my horse," Fargo said.

"You're forgetting the gentleman who ambushed you on the way here," Quilby said. "He's still locked up at the jail and hasn't been fed or given anything to drink."

"He's your problem."

"How so? It's you he tried to kill. And I made it clear when you arrived that we no longer have a lawman. I'm afraid the responsibility of what to do with him rests on your shoulders."

"Hell," Fargo said.

"You can tie him and bring him along and turn him over to the marshal in Silver Creek, although I doubt he'd have jurisdiction since his only extends to the town limits and the crime wasn't committed there."

"Or I could leave him in the cell to rot."

Quilby grinned. "Could you really? Are you *that* hard?"

"According to you I am."

"You should be flattered that you're known for your grit. Most men aren't nearly as tough as you."

"If you say so."

"Let me know what you decide to do with whatever his name was." Quilby smiled and walked off.

Fargo stood debating. He would just as soon leave Chester Leghorny behind bars. So what if the yack starved to death? But it wasn't in his nature. With a sigh, he headed for the jail.

A surprise awaited him. The front door was open. He entered

and received a second jolt. The cell door was open, too, and the key in the lock.

Chester was nowhere to be seen.

"Son of a bitch."

Fargo supposed it was possible that Leghorny had somehow snagged the key off the peg. Perhaps by using his belt. He walked over and took the key out and turned to hang it on the peg.

A man he'd never set eyes on before rose from behind the desk with a scattergun leveled. Short and squat, he was a sloppy dresser and crowned his head with a narrow-brimmed hat. He grinned at how clever he'd been and said, "So much as twitch and I blow you in half."

From behind the open front door stepped a nervous Chester Leghorny. He glanced into the street, quickly closed the door, and pulled the shade. Only then did he say, "I bet you feel plumb stupid."

"I walked right into it," Fargo admitted. He was focused on the hand cannon. One blast and he'd be in pieces.

"Where's Nevada?" the man with the scattergun growled.

"Who?" Fargo said.

"My pard. He went to the whore's to do you in. He was to meet me here when he got done. But if you're here and he ain't, that must mean you did him in. Which makes me powerful mad." The man raised the scattergun.

6

Fargo tensed to make a desperate stab for his Colt. He couldn't possibly clear leather before the killer fired, but he would try to get off a shot.

A reprieve came from an unlikely source. "Hold on, Merkham," Chester Leghorny said. "People will hear and come runnin'."

"Who cares?" Merkham replied, but he didn't shoot.

"They might see us leavin'," Chester said.

"So what?"

"So they're headin' for Silver Creek, aren't they? So maybe they'd tell Marshal Sadler."

"He won't be able to prove anything," Merkham said.

"Maybe not," Chester said. "But why not do this smart and take Fargo off in the woods where no one can see or hear?"

"I suppose that makes more sense," Merkham reluctantly agreed. To Fargo he said, "Turn around and reach for the ceiling."

Fargo swiveled on his bootheels and raised his arms.

"Get over there and take his Colt," Merkham said.

"Why me?" Chester asked.

"Because I have him covered, and you don't. Do it careful, and don't get between us. I wouldn't want to blow you apart if I have to cut loose on him."

"Why don't I cover him, and you take his six-shooter?"

"Do as I told you, damn it," Merkham snapped, "before someone walks in on us."

Chester muttered, and Fargo heard the scrape of boots.

"Don't you try anything," Chester warned him, "or I'll duck and let Merkham take you all at the hips."

"Quit jabbering, and do it," Merkham said.

The scrapes came closer. Fargo gauged that Chester was slightly to his right. He was tempted to glance over his shoulder but didn't want to give his intentions away.

"What are you waiting for?" Merkham demanded.

"Just making sure he's behavin'," Chester said.

"You're spineless, is what you are. I've heard you were, and now I know. It's a wonder Hardy put up with you."

"No need to insult me."

"Leghorny, by-God, if you don't take that damn Colt of his right this instant, I'll shoot you."

"All right, all right," Chester said angrily.

Fargo felt fingers brush his holster. Whirling and sidestepping to put Chester between him and Merkham, he shoved Chester at the scattergun-wielding assassin.

Chester stumbled and almost fell.

Merkham, eager to shoot, angrily shouted, "Chester, damn you! Get out of the way!"

By then Fargo had his Colt out. He fanned the hammer twice. Merkham was knocked back but stayed on his feet and pointed the scattergun. Fargo dived at the floor. He was in midair when the twin barrels boomed. He figured the spread would catch him full-on but Merkham fired high and blistered the air above him. Fargo crashed to the floor and rolled.

Merkham frantically tried to reload.

Taking aim, Fargo shot him in the forehead. Merkham's head snapped back, and his mouth worked wordlessly, and he melted.

Chester had frozen in fear. The spell broke, and he bleated like a stricken lamb and backed off with his hands out. "Don't shoot! Don't shoot!"

As much as Fargo would've liked to, instead, he growled, "On your belly on the floor. Now."

"Whatever you say," Chester said, dropping so quickly and so hard, it was a wonder he didn't hurt himself. "You don't have to tell me twice."

Fargo stepped to Merkham and nudged him with a boot. As if there was any doubt.

"God," Chester said, "you killed him."

"No fooling," Fargo said. "Now, what to do about you?"

From outside came yells and a commotion, and the front door was thrown open. Arthur Thomas and two others filled the doorway but didn't enter. "We heard shots," the treasurer said.

"It was another try on my life," Fargo said. "Do any of you know this man?" He motioned at Merkham.

Arthur Thomas shook his head and swallowed. "I never saw the gentleman before."

"He's not from Lodestone," a man said.

Fargo indicated Chester. "This one says he was hired in Silver Creek. Why would anyone there want me dead?"

"I'm sure I don't know," Arthur Thomas said. He bobbed his chin at Chester. "Has he given you a reason?"

"He says he doesn't know why they want me bucked out."

The treasurer did a strange thing. He smiled. "Ah, well," he said, "in that case, we're all in the dark. We'll leave you to dispose of that body and deal with your prisoner."

"I'm not an undertaker," Fargo said. As far as he was concerned, Merkham could lie there and rot.

"Neither are we," Arthur Thomas said. He smiled again, and he and the townsmen departed.

"I wouldn't trust him if I were you," Chester remarked. "I don't think he was tellin' the truth."

"Listen to the kettle," Fargo said.

"You've spared me twice now," Chester replied. "That's more than anybody has done for me in a coon's age. From here on out, I'll be as honest with you as I'd be with my ma."

"Does she live in Silver Creek?"

"Ma? No. What'd make you think that? She went to her reward pretty near ten years ago. But I was always honest with her when she was breathin'."

Fargo went to the front window, raised the shade, and peered out.

Down the street, Arthur Thomas was in an animated conversation with Mayor Quilby and Gladiola Thimblebottom. Gladiola looked mad. She kept flapping her flabby arm in the direction of the jail.

"What do you see?" Chester asked.

"None of your business." Fargo saw Gladiola grab the mayor by the front of his shirt. To his amazement, Quilby cringed.

"Why are you bein' so mean?" Chester asked.

"I'm not all that fond of gents who hire out to kill me," Fargo answered. Outside, Gladiola had let go of the mayor. She jabbed a thick finger at him and at the treasurer and said something that made both men scowl. Then she stomped off.

"That was before I got to know you," Chester was saying. "Now that I do, I've had me a brainstorm."

"You need a brain for that."

"I have a thinker like everybody else. And mine tells me that we should partner up."

Fargo turned and stared.

"Don't look at me like that. I can help you."

"By shooting me in the back?"

"A fella makes one mistake and you hold it against him forever. No, I can help you by findin' out stuff. I'm real sneaky that way."

"You're sneaky pretty much every way," Fargo said.

Chester Leghorny beamed. "Why, that's about the nicest thing anybody ever said to me. I suppose I am, at that. When I was little, I'd sneak cookies and sugar and my ma's garters all the time."

"Your ma's garters?"

"To use as a slingshot. You hook them to a forked stick and you can wallop birds and the like."

"Killed a lot, did you?"

"Not any. The slingshot wasn't that powerful. Who'd want to kill sweet little birdies, anyway? I sure wouldn't."

33

"Yet you hired out as an assassin."

"Don't start with that again. I became an assassin by accident."

Fargo walked over and hunkered and peered into Chester's eyes. As near as he could tell, it wasn't an act.

"What are you doin'?"

"Looking for that brain you claim you have."

"That's plumb silly. A man's brain is inside his head. How are you goin' to see through skin and bone? My brain is in there. I feel it sometimes."

"You feel your brain?"

"When I'm drunk I feel it the most because it hurts. But I also feel it sometimes when I'm tryin' to think. Of course, I don't try to think too often because as near as I can tell, nothin' good ever came of it."

Fargo grabbed him by the arm and hauled him to his feet.

"Careful. That hurts. You're a lot stronger than you must think you are or you wouldn't be squeezin' so hard."

"I have a deal for you," Fargo said.

Chester grinned happily. "Name it, pard. It's as good as done, or my last name ain't Leghorny."

"The deal is this. I'll let you go if you promise to ride out of town and never let me set eyes on you again."

"But we're pards now."

"No," Fargo said, "we're not. I'm by my lonesome and you're an idiot. Take your horse and go anywhere you want and count yourself lucky that I believe you're as stupid as you act."

"That was mean."

"Yes or no?"

"If I say no?"

"I throw you back in the cell and throw away the key."

"I guess it has to be yes. But between you and me, you might try eatin' more pie."

"Pie?" Fargo said.

Chester nodded. "To sweeten your disposition. When I was little, a piece of pie always cheered me up. It would do the same for you. I don't know if anyone has ever told you, but you can be grumpy."

Fargo pointed at the front door. "Scat."

"Right this second?"

"Light a shuck."

"Don't I get to eat first? I haven't had a bite since yesterday. Hardy and Wilson were in a hurry to get here and kill you. I told them how hungry I was. Heck, they could hear my stomach growlin'. But they didn't care. Those two weren't as fond of food as I am. To them it was just somethin' to shove into their mouths now and then. Me, I've always thought food was special. Without it, what would we eat?"

Fargo gripped him by the shirt.

"Here we go again," Chester said.

Pulling him to the front door, Fargo opened it. "If you know what's good for you, you'll take the hint."

"Which one? You've given me five or six."

"This," Fargo said, and pushed him.

Chester tottered back and fell against the hitch rail.

"I don't ever want to see you again."

"You don't mean that, pard."

"Get this through your noggin. We are not pards. We will never be pards. Savvy?"

"Maybe you should try cake instead of pie," Chester said. "There's more sugar in cake and you can stand to be sweeter."

"I could just shoot you." Fargo slammed the door and moved to the window.

Chester saw him and sadly shook his head. "All right. I'm goin'. But you're makin' a mistake. Sooner or later you'll need me to back you and the only back you'll have will be your own."

Fargo motioned sharply for Chester to start walking.

"Are you sure? This is your last chance to change your mind."

Fargo placed his hand on his Colt.

"There you go again," Chester said. "But you know what? I think you really don't mean it. I think you want me to find out who hired me and why. And when I have, I'll let you know, so you can settle their hash. I'd do it myself, but I ain't much good at hash-settlin'."

"Just go!" Fargo shouted.

"See? That didn't sound sincere." Chester looked around, then came to the window and lowered his voice. "I do savvy, after all. You want to give everyone the idea we've split up when we really haven't. Don't worry. I won't give it away. I'm good at bein' sneaky, remember?"

"I don't know how else to say this," Fargo said. "Get the hell lost."

Chester grinned and winked. "If that's the way you want to be, fine."

"Honest to God," Fargo said.

Turning his head from side to side, Chester hollered so anyone could hear. "From this moment on, we're quits. It's every hombre for himself." He winked again and said quietly, "I'll be the best pard you've ever had. Just you wait and see." Hooking his thumbs in his belt, he sauntered off.

"God help me," Fargo said.

7

The saloon had customers.

Fargo bought a bottle, carried it to a table, and set to drinking and playing cards with several townsmen who were packed and ready to go and were celebrating with a last fling.

They greeted him with smiles. One man mentioned how glad he was that Fargo had agreed to guide them and the others nodded.

It amused Fargo, them making such a fuss over so short a journey. "We should be safe enough," he cracked. "It's not as if we'll be in danger of dying of hunger or thirst."

"It's not any of that we're worried about," an older man remarked, drawing sharp stares from the rest.

"I reckon the bears and mountain lions will leave us alone, too," Fargo said.

"Not them, neither." The older man told him. He was half in his cups and had a vacant expression.

"That's enough, Edgar," another man said.

"What did I do?" Edgar asked.

"The scout doesn't want to hear that you're afraid of wasps and such," another townsman said.

"Wasps? Hell," Edgar said, "when I get stung I hardly ever feel it."

"You'll feel my boot up your ass," the same man said.

Fargo was surprised at how angry the other men were. "It's nothing to get mad about."

"You don't know Edgar like we do," one said. "He never can watch that tongue of his."

Edgar had been examining his cards but now he set them down and stabbed a finger at each of his companions. "You and you and you leave me be. I don't have a leaky mouth."

"You should shut up now," one said.

"Go to hell and take her and him with you," Edgar said.

"Her and him?" Fargo repeated, and didn't know what to make of the worried looks that came over the others.

"Or him and her," Edgar said, and tittered as if it were funny.

"Pay Edgar no mind, mister," a man said. "He's always going on about things that make no sense."

"I do not," Edgar said indignantly. "I have as much sense as anybody."

Just then the batwings parted and in walked Mayor Quilby and Arthur Thomas.

They made for the bar but Quilby looked over at Fargo's table and caught on right away that something was going on. He veered over and Thomas tagged along.

"Hello, Fred," the mayor said to one of the men. "Why do you look so mad?"

"Edgar, here, is flapping his gums," Fred said.

"Oh?"

Befuddled by drink, Edgar blinked a few times and said, "Why, look who it is. The 'him' himself."

"How's that again?" Mayor Quilby asked.

"Nothing," Edgar said, and laughed.

"He's drunk," Arthur Thomas said. "Someone should see that he gets home safely."

"Home?" Edgar said. "It's not my home no more. I have a new home waiting in Silver Creek. We all do."

"Yes," Mayor Quilby said, "and we want to be on our best behavior when we get there. So no drinking for you along the way."

"Best behavior?" Edgar said. He found that funny, too. "What will she do? Curtsy and say 'pretty please'?"

"That's enough," Quilby said.

"Indeed, it is." Arthur Thomas moved around the table. "On your feet, Edgar. I'm taking you home right this minute."

"No," Fargo said. "You're not."

Everyone froze.

"Edgar," Fargo said, bending toward him, "who is this 'she' you keep talking about? What's going on here?"

Only then did Edgar notice the glares the other men were giving him. He coughed and fidgeted and shook his head. "Nothing.

Like they said, I've had too much to drink." He suddenly pushed to his feet. "It's best I be going."

"Go with him, Arthur," the mayor said. "Make sure he gets there."

"I'll take him," Fargo said. He was damned curious about what was going on and it would give him a chance to question Edgar more.

"That's not necessary," said a new voice, and Gladiola Thimblebottom moved around them and over behind Edgar.

Fargo was as taken aback as the others. He hadn't heard her come in.

"Gladiola!" Quilby exclaimed. "You shouldn't be in here. A saloon is no place for a lady."

"Why, Mayor Quilby," she said, "I thank you for your concern for my reputation. But everyone knows me well enough to know I *am* a lady. I happened to be passing by and overheard a few remarks." She put a hand on Edgar's shoulder. "I agree you should be escorted home. And I'm the one who will do it."

Fargo didn't like her tone. He should've let it drop, but he said, "We'll both go with him."

"What?" Mayor Quilby said.

"Why bother yourself?" Arthur Thomas said.

"It's no bother." Fargo pushed back his chair. "Count me out of this hand, boys. But save my chair. I'll be back."

"Really, Mr. Fargo," Mayor Quilby said. "I insist you stay and have a good time. Gladiola can handle Edgar."

"It's Miss Thimblebottom to you," Gladiola said.

Quilby swallowed. "Certainly. Sorry. I forgot myself."

"There's a lot of that going around," Gladiola said. "It's why I'm keeping an eye on things."

"On what exactly?" Fargo asked.

"You know," she said.

"Make it plainer," Fargo said.

Gladiola's moon face cragged with resentment. "I don't very much like being told what to do. But for your information, I'm keeping an eye on the preparations, of course."

"Of course," Mayor Quilby echoed. "She's one of our leading citizens and has more riding on the move than most."

"That's enough," Gladiola said.

Fargo remembered her grabbing the mayor by the shirt earlier and how Quilby hadn't lifted a finger to stop her. He began to wonder who really ran the town. "Let's tend to Edgar, so I can return to my card game."

"You wouldn't have to return if you didn't go," Gladiola said, "but very well."

With an unexpected display of strength, she gripped Edgar by the shoulders and raised him out of his chair. She didn't pull him up. She *lifted* him.

Edgar appeared petrified. "I can find my way my own self," he said anxiously. "There's no need to put yourself to any bother, Miss Thimblebottom."

"It's no bother at all," Gladiola said in a way that suggested it was a whole lot of bother. She turned Edgar toward the batwings. "Gentlemen first," she said, and gave him a push.

Edgar tripped and almost pitched to his knees.

Fargo followed them out. He didn't know what to make of it all. Gladiola was throwing her more than considerable weight around as if she were in charge. That the mayor let her cow him, and that old Edgar was afraid of her, would have been comical if not for the fact that they were trying to hide something. But what? he wondered, and caught up to them. "Nice night."

Gladiola crooked her thick neck to stare at the stars. "I hadn't noticed." She looked at him. "You don't need to walk with us."

"I can use the fresh air," Fargo said. "How about you, Edgar? Is the air helping to clear your head?"

"Some," Edgar said sullenly.

"What worries you about the wagon trip to Silver Creek?" Fargo asked.

"Who said anything does?"

"You did."

Edgar gave Gladiola a quick glance and faced front again. "I was tipsy. I didn't know what I was saying."

"It's good of you to admit it," Gladiola said.

"I don't want to cause no trouble," Edgar said. "And I'm sorry for inconveniencing you. Powerful sorry."

"It's no inconvenience at all," Gladiola said sweetly. "What are friends for?"

The town was unnaturally still. Most of the windows were dark, a testament to how many businesses were empty and houses deserted.

"I hear tell this was a lively town before the ore ran out," Fargo remarked.

"Was it ever," Gladiola said. "A dozen saloons were going, not just the one. And there were always people out and about."

"What is it you did here?"

"I was one of the leading lights, you might say," Gladiola said. "I ran a number of enterprises."

"She ran whores, mostly," Edgar said.

Gladiola's fist was a blur. She struck Edger in the middle of his back and he cried out and stumbled. "That's enough out of you."

"You're a madam?" Fargo said.

"What of it?"

Fargo grinned. "I like a bawdy house as much as the next gent. Where did all your fallen angels get to?"

"Look around you. The work dried up. A lot of my gals headed for Denver. Once I'm set up in Silver Creek, I'll send for them."

Fargo recollected hearing that Silver Creek was more strait-laced than Lodestone. "They might not take kindly to a whore-house."

"What they do or don't take kindly to won't matter," Gladiola declared. "When I set my mind to something, I do it."

"Does she ever," Edgar said.

"I told you to shush."

"Will you trounce him like you threatened to trounce me?" Fargo brought up.

"You don't think I can?"

Fargo bit off a chuckle. The notion was preposterous. All he said was "Why would you want to?"

"When I rely on someone to get something done, I expect it to *get* done," Gladiola said. "I don't like failure and I don't accept excuses."

"I'm not one to make any."

"That's good to hear. I don't think you realize how important this is. Not just to me but to everyone who's left. We're counting on starting over in Silver Creek, come hell or high water."

"All I care about is getting you there," Fargo said. Their plans for the future couldn't interest him less.

Gladiola didn't seem to hear him. "It was a terrible stroke of luck, the gold running out just when things were going so grand. Another couple of years and we'd have been rich. Some of us, any-way."

"You hope to get rich in Silver Creek?"

"Why not? Their silver mine, a geologist fella said, could last a hundred years or more. They have a whole mountain veined with the stuff." Gladiola paused. "Those who run things there stand to be as wealthy as we would have been here."

"I've never much cared about being rich," Fargo admitted.

"Then you're a fool. Money is everything. It's power. It's luxuries. It's doing as we damn well please."

"I do as I please anyway."

"You're one of those," Gladiola said.

"Which?" Fargo said.

"You have no perception. You think being carefree is all that counts. You don't look past the next whiskey bottle or the next card game. Life for you is an amusement, nothing more."

Fargo had to admit she was partly right. "I also like bare-naked ladies."

Gladiola didn't smile. "People like you are too dumb to know they're being lorded over. The rich and powerful control things. Always have, always will. And I aim to be one of them."

"And control Silver Creek?"

"Why not? I have as—" Gladiola caught herself, and frowned. "You ask too damn many questions."

A troubling thought occurred to Fargo. "Do the people of Silver Creek know that all of you are moving there?"

Gladiola hesitated. "Who can say?"

"They might not like the idea."

"Who cares whether they do, or they don't. We're going, and that's that."

Fargo decided to come right out with it. "Is there more to this than you've been telling me?"

"I'm sure I don't know what you mean. You were hired to do a job. That's all there is to it, as far as you're concerned." Gladiola gave Edgar another push. "Now go back to the goddamn saloon where you belong and quit pestering me."

Fargo stopped. He had gotten as much out of her as he was going to. He watched her waddle into the night with a feeling taking root that the attempts on his life were harbingers of worse to come.

8

It was laughter that woke Fargo. He rolled over and wondered what he was doing in a strange bed in a room that smelled faintly of lavender and recollected the mayor saying he could sleep in a vacant house for the night. Sitting up, he saw his gun belt and hat and boots on the floor, where he must have dropped them. He recalled playing poker until midnight and downing a bottle of red-eye. The whiskey explained the slight throbbing in his temples, although usually it took a lot more than one bottle to have that effect.

Only as he slid his legs over the side did he realize he was holding his Colt. At least he'd had the presence of mind to not be unarmed. He stretched and smacked his dry lips and went to stand and bumped something that skittered across the floor.

The empty bottle.

Fargo picked up his gun belt and shoved the Colt into the holster. He dressed, strapped the gun belt around his waist, and peered out the window.

The citizens of Lodestone had been as good as their word. Their wagons were lined up along the Main Street, ready to depart at ten. They were in good spirits and making quite a racket with their cheerful yelling back and forth.

Turning, Fargo jingled down a flight of stairs. He was halfway to the front door when it opened, and who should bustle in but the lady in red, herself.

"The mayor sent me to see if you were awake," Hortense said. She had on a different dress. One more fitting for a proper lady than the lacier outfit she'd worn when they'd met. "What are you looking at? As if I can't guess."

Fargo grasped her wrist and pulled her against him. She didn't resist. He kicked the door shut and pressed her to a wall and said, "Guess what I'd like for breakfast."

42

"You're serious?"

Fargo took her hand and placed it on his hardening pole. "As serious as a redwood."

"Oh my." Hortense laughed, then glanced at the door. "What if someone comes?"

"I'll shoot them."

"I don't know how long we have."

"Ever hear of a fast one?" Fargo leaned in and licked her earlobe and her neck and she wriggled invitingly.

"How fast?" Hortense asked.

"Then you're interested?" Fargo commenced to hike up her dress.

"You're taking a lot for granted," Hortense said with another glance at the door. "But, Lordy, yes. I am."

"That's all I wanted to hear." Bunching the folds of her skirt, Fargo raised it above her waist. Underneath, she wore a white cotton chemise. He bunched that, too, exposing the silken sweep of her thighs.

Hortense kissed his cheek and his neck and said huskily, "I haven't had it in the daytime in a while."

"You're having it now," Fargo said. He tugged on his gun belt, and once it was high enough, he undid his pants belt, so he could free his manhood.

Hortense glanced down and smiled. "Oh my. It's as big as I remember." She spread her legs and looked him in the eyes. "You'd better get to it, handsome."

"I aim to please, ma'am," Fargo said, and without any foreplay, without even reaching down to align his pole with her slit, he inserted the tip, grinned, and rammed up into her.

Hortense threw her head back and opened her mouth to cry out but caught herself. Instead, she gasped and buried her face in his shoulder. "Ohhhh," she groaned. "You feel so good."

Fargo levered onto the tips of his toes. Her soft sheath clung to him like wet satin and she raised her legs and wrapped them around his waist, locking her feet behind him.

"You call this quick?"

Fargo rocked on the balls of his feet, moving faster, ever faster, until in no time, the two of them were breathlessly panting and he was slamming her against the wall with each thrust of his hips.

"Yes," Hortense said. "Oh, yes."

The pain in Fargo's temples was fading, replaced by a familiar constriction. He cupped her bottom and squeezed a breast and was close to going over the brink.

Hortense went into a carnal frenzy, moving up and down to match his tempo, and uttered little mewing noises.

A shadow passed across a window in the parlor, but as near as Fargo could tell, it wasn't anything to be concerned about. His legs became twin steam-engine pistons and he put the window and the door and everything else from his mind except for the sensations she provoked.

"Ahhhhh," Hortense exclaimed, her breath warm on his throat. Bowing her head, she closed her eyes and said, "I'm there! I'm there!"

Her explosion shook both of them.

Fargo held on tight as, the very next moment, his own occurred. The two of them thrashed and bucked in abandon. Together, they crested. Together, they coasted to a stop and collapsed against each other, with Hortense sucking in air while digging her fingernails into his shoulders.

"You were magnificent."

Fargo grunted.

"I mean it. I don't say that often."

Fargo had been with enough doves to know not to take their compliments seriously. "If you say so," he said, and began to ease out of her.

"Wait," Hortense said. She closed her eyes and gave him a last squeeze, low down.

"I'm obliged, ma'am," Fargo said with a grin.

"Such formality from a gentleman who has screwed my brains out," Hortense said.

"Tomorrow night on the trail we can do it again."

"You wish," Hortense said. "There will be too many folks about. We can't just walk off together."

"Why not? It's what you do."

"At the saloon I did," Hortense said. "But she might not take kindly to me flaunting it along the way."

Fargo was pulling out of her. " 'She'?" he said.

"The woman I work for."

"Let me guess." Taking a step back, Fargo pulled his britches up. "Gladiola Thimblebottom."

"None other," Hortense confirmed. "She ran every dove in Lodestone and will run me in Silver Creek, too."

"You don't mind?"

"Why should I? Her cut is fair, and she looks after her girls. You should have seen how sad she was when she had to let nearly all of them go because of Lodestone failing. But she has big plans, that lady."

"Does she now?" Fargo said.

"She never lets anything keep her down. When she sets her mind to something, she does it. And she has her mind set on putting together the same setup she had here over in Silver Creek. They might not like it much, but there's nothing they can do to stop her."

"The people in Silver Creek know that she aims to start up a whorehouse?"

Hortense was putting herself together and answered absently, "Somehow they got word that we're coming, and what we're up to. By 'we' I mean all of us, not just Gladiola. She told me that she and the mayor suspect there's a traitor among us."

"A traitor?"

Hortense nodded while smoothing her dress. "Someone who knew about the town meetings we'd held about going there. The next we knew, we got word from them to stay away."

"You don't say."

"Who do they think they are, anyhow?" Hortense said. "The mayor and the town council there think they have the right to keep us out, but they don't. This is America. People can go where they want and do as they please."

"How far do you reckon they'd go to stop you?"

Hortense looked up. "How do you mean?"

"The assassins who keep trying to kill me," Fargo reminded her. "It could be you've given me the answer to why."

"Silver Creek hired them? How come? To stop you from taking us there?" Hortense gnawed her lip. "That doesn't make sense. As you pointed out, it's only fifty miles. We could go there our own selves, only the mayor insisted we needed you."

Fargo had a lot to ponder, but it would have to wait. Moving to the front door, he opened it for her.

As Hortense sashayed past, she caressed his chin. "By the way, thank you. That was a wonderful way to start the day."

"Remember what I said about the stopover."

"I'll keep it in mind but don't hold your breath."

As they approached the wagons, Fargo became the focus of attention. The mayor spotted him, and he and several others hurried to meet him. So did Gladiola Thimblebottom and Mouse, the stableman.

"I hope you slept well," Mayor Quilby said. "It promises to be a long day."

"In more ways than one," Arthur Thomas said.

Fargo didn't want to get Hortense into trouble by mentioning what she had told him. But he did want to find out more, so he casually remarked, "By the way, how do the folks in Silver Creek feel about you moving there?"

All of them except Mouse got the look deer did when they blundered into the light of a campfire at night.

"I doubt they know we're coming," Arthur Thomas said.

"It's not as if we advertised it in their newspaper," Mayor Quilby said.

"But if they did know?" Fargo didn't let them off the hook.

Quilby shrugged. "I'd imagine they'd welcome us with open arms. We're Lodestone's leading citizens. We'd be a positive addition to any community."

"And if they don't like it, so what?" Gladiola Thimblebottom said. "They have no legal right to stop us."

"None whatsoever," the mayor quickly agreed.

"We're goin', and that's that," Mouse said.

Mayor Quilby took a pocket watch from his vest pocket and consulted it. "Ten minutes until we head out. I can't wait."

"I'll fetch my horse and be right back," Fargo said. He had stabled the stallion the night before. It didn't take long to bring it out of the stall and saddle up. He was about to climb on when someone hissed at him from behind. Whirling, he dropped his hand to his Colt.

"*Pssssst*. Over here! It's me."

A head poked out of another stall.

"Chester?" Fargo said.

Chester Leghorny glanced out at the townspeople and the wagons and put a finger to his lips. "Not so loud. Do you want them to hear you?" He crooked the same finger. "I've found out some things, like I promised I would."

Fargo let the reins dangle and went over. "I'd almost forgotten about you," he admitted.

"How can you forget your own pard?"

"What have you been up to?"

"Bein' sneaky," Chester said. "Listenin' at peepholes and watchin' who goes where and does what. And I heard somethin' interestin'. Somethin' you need to know."

"I'm listening."

"I was over at the mayor's house last night, and the parlor window was open," Chester related. "Him and some of the others were talkin' "—he paused—"about you."

"Do tell."

Chester bobbed his chin. "That big gal, the one that's built like a barn, was sayin' as how she didn't like you much."

"Gladiola Thimblebottom."

"That's the one," Chester said, and laughed. "Can you imagine havin' a last name like 'Thimblebottom'? You'd be a laughing-stock."

"A gent with the name 'Leghorny' has no room to talk," Fargo said.

"Are you pokin' fun at me? Because if you are, I can stop right now, and you can find out what I found out your own self."

"Keep talking."

"No more pokin' fun, you hear? A person can't help the name they're born with. It ought to be that they let you pick your own. But how can you do that when you're a baby? Everybody would be called ga-ga and goo-goo and that'd be silly as could be, wouldn't it?"

"There's a lot of that going around these days."

"A lot of what?"

"Silly."

"I haven't noticed much of it, but if you say so, fine. All I'm sayin' is that if I'd gotten to name myself, I'd have a great last name. Somethin' like Lincoln or Washington or Stubbendorf."

"Stubbendorf?"

"I heard that once. Some German guy, it was. Best name, ever."

"Chester?"

"Yes, sir?"

"What the hell did you hear?"

"Oh. After that barn lady said she didn't like you, she told those others it was a good thing she didn't, because now she had no regrets about paintin' a target on your back."

"What did the others do?"

"That was the strange part," Chester said. "They laughed."

9

The first few miles were as easy as anything.

The road was more than wide enough, and there hadn't been any rain in weeks so they didn't have to worry about becoming stuck.

Fargo discovered that nearly all the wagons were overloaded. That was typical. He didn't make an issue of it, though, not when they had only fifty miles to travel. On a longer trek across desert or in wet country, he would have.

The mayor and everyone else gave him a lot of smiles and treated him as friendly as could be.

Fargo wasn't fooled. They were using him. He was sure of it now. They hadn't hired him for his scouting skills. Not those alone, anyhow. He suspected another reason, and the more he thought about it, the madder he became. Simmering, he bided his time until he could get to the truth.

To the north and south rose lofty peaks. Miles high, for most of the year they were crowned with white mantles. In the heat of summer, with the snow melted, bare rock glinted dully.

The Rockies were in full bloom. Aspen leaves shimmered in the breeze and ranks of firs stood at attention. High country meadows broke the tracts of woodland with wildflowers and waving grass.

At that altitude mule deer were more common than their white-tailed cousins. Elk rested in thick cover during the day and came out in early morning and evening to graze. Out on the plains a goodly number of bears had been exterminated but up here they were plentiful, both grizzlies and black bears.

Smaller game was abundant but elusive. Rabbits bounded off in alarm. Squirrels peered at the clattering Conestogas and flatbeds from high perches and now and then chittered their annoyance. Chipmunks, too, didn't take kindly to the invasion.

Fargo drank it all in. As much as he liked a glass of whiskey and four of a kind at cards and the silken feel of a woman's thighs, he liked the wilds more. They were a tonic he couldn't get enough of.

Early on, he rode at the head of the train. After the first few miles, when the road narrowed, he rode back along the line, noting who was where and paying no mind to their false smiles. When he came to the last wagon and reined around to go to the front, he heard a hiss.

Pines bordered the road at that point, and in among them, riding merrily along on a sorrel, was Chester Leghorny. He grinned and waved.

Fargo checked that none of the drivers or riders were looking back at him and reined into the trees. "What are you doing here?" he demanded.

"What does it look like, pard?" Chester said, sounding surprised at the question. "Goin' to Silver Creek with you."

"I told you in Lodestone that you should go your own way."

"Yes, you did," Chester said, "which I thought was a fine how-do-you-do after I spied on those folks for you."

"Chester . . ."

Chester held up a hand. "You didn't really think I'd go off and leave you? A man doesn't do that to his pard."

"Stop calling me that."

"It's what we are, isn't it? I've hitched my wagon to yours and will be your pard for as long as you'll have me."

"You've done enough."

"Not nearly," Chester said. "Not after I'd hired out to do you in. I have a lot to make up for."

Fargo sighed.

"I won't be any bother. They won't know I'm along. I'll stay hid in the woods and spy on them like I did in town."

"Two hundred and fifty dollars," Fargo said.

"What about it?"

"That's how much I'll give you to turn around and head for Denver and let me handle this myself."

Chester jutted his jaw in indignation. "What kind of pard would I be if I ran out on you for money?"

"You were willing to kill me for money."

"That was different. I didn't know you then. And they never did pay us, so there really wasn't any money involved."

"Three hundred dollars."

"No."

"Five hundred."

Chester whistled. "That's a lot. It shows how highly you think of me. Which would make it even worse if I left."

"Why is it," Fargo said, "that when I talk to you, I always end up talking in circles?"

"Beats me, pard," Chester said. "I talk in straight lines, myself. Or maybe squares or those longer squares. Fact is, I'm not much at shapes."

"Do you happen to have a bottle in your saddlebags?"

"Sure don't. Why?"

"Pity," Fargo said, and raised his reins. "If I can't stop you from tagging along, at least be careful. Whoever is out to kill me might do the same to you if they think you're helping me."

"Don't fret, pard," Chester said, and patted his six-shooter. "I've never shot anybody, but that doesn't mean I won't if I have to, and they give me time to do it."

"God," Fargo said.

"What?"

Fargo shook his head and gigged the Ovaro to the road. He moved from wagon to wagon and was about midway when a husky voice called out to him.

"Hold on there, handsome."

Fargo slowed to pace the wagon. "You're a lady of many talents."

Perched on the seat, her knees spread and the reins dangling between them, Hortense chuckled. "There's not much to it. The team does all the work."

"You didn't hire one of the men to do it for you?"

Inside the wagon someone said, "Why should I do that when Hortense already works for me?" Gladiola Thimblebottom eased her girth from under the canvas and roosted next to Hortense, who had to slide to an end to make room. "I've been meaning to talk to you."

"Oh?" Fargo said. He'd as soon haul her off the Conestoga and punch her in the mouth. It was a shame she was female.

"I've heard about the tries on your life," Gladiola said. "You'd better keep your eyes peeled. There might be more."

"What makes you say that?" Fargo pretended it hadn't occurred to him, and then couldn't resist adding, "It's not as if someone painted a target on my back."

Gladiola gave a mild start, then composed herself and replied, "No, it's sure not. But somebody is clearly up to no good."

"I wonder who."

"You ask me, it's someone in Silver Creek. Someone who doesn't want you to take us there."

"Seems a silly reason to want me dead," Fargo said.

"You never know with people. They do peculiar things. Just don't let them make wolf bait of you."

"Why, Gladiola," Fargo said. "I didn't know you cared."

"I don't," she said flatly, "except insofar as I had a say in the decision to hire you and don't want you bucked out before we get there."

"You're all heart." Fargo almost said, "and a lot of lard, besides," but he touched his hat brim and rode on up the line. When he got to the front, he found two riders waiting for him.

"There you are," Mayor Quilby said. "We'd like a few words." The mayor was a terrible rider. He flounced with every stride his horse took and clung to the saddle horn, even though his mount was moving at a walk.

"That we would," Arthur Thomas said.

"It's my day for words," Fargo told them. "What's on your minds?"

"We have a feeling there could be trouble along the way," Quilby said. "Call it a premonition, if you like."

"Yes, a premonition," the treasurer echoed.

"We wanted to warn you so you can be on your guard," Quilby said. "It wouldn't do for you to come to harm."

"Or for any of you," Fargo said.

"That goes without saying," Mayor Quilby said. "We hired you, after all. Our lives are of paramount importance."

"Not that yours isn't," Arthur Thomas said.

Fargo had to get out of there. "I reckon I'll ride on ahead. If you hear shots, stop and be ready for anything."

"You should take someone with you," Mayor Quilby advised.

"No." Fargo was sick of the whole bunch. They were playing him for a fool, and he resented it. He tapped his spurs and trotted around several bends. When next he glanced back, he was out of their sight. "Good riddance," he grumbled, and slowed.

The road climbed. Eventually it would bring them to Smith Pass, named after an early mountain man. Once over the Divide, it was downhill all the way to Silver Creek.

An ambush could come at any time. The woods were heavy enough to hide a small army. Anyone using the road would be a sitting duck.

Fargo had keener eyes than most when it came to spotting skulkers. He'd whetted his talents against the likes of the Apaches

51

and the Sioux, where if a man didn't learn quick, he'd end up staked out for ants or scalped.

Ahead, the road narrowed to where it was barely wide enough for a wagon. Hoofprints pockmarked it. A lot of traffic had passed up and down in recent years. Smith Pass wasn't just for Silver Creek's benefit. It gave access to the whole west side of the range.

The sharp cry of a jay drew Fargo's gaze to a cluster of blue spruce. Jays squawked a lot. It was nothing unusual. But this one was fluttering back and forth over a particular spot and looking down at something on the ground. A bobcat, maybe, Fargo figured, under the tree where the jays had their nest.

Then a human head appeared and turned in his direction. So did a rifle barrel.

Exploding into motion, Fargo reined into the trees on the other side of the road just as the rifle banged. Lead struck a trunk and sent slivers flying. He swept around a spruce and then another and on past a thicket and drew rein. Vaulting down, he shucked his Henry from the scabbard and ran to a small tree and flattened. Wriggling under its low branches, he took off his hat and set it beside him.

The smart thing was to make the shooter come to him. Or there could be more than one.

The wait seemed endless.

Fargo was tired of being a target. He made up his mind to do something about it. He'd have to hold off until they crossed the Divide—and manage to stay alive until then.

Movement brought his musing to an end. A furtive form was gliding from tree to tree. Seconds later another appeared. They were about twenty yards apart, close enough that they could cover each other.

Fargo trained the Henry and pressed his cheek to the brass receiver. He'd spared Chester but he'd be damned if he'd spare this pair. If not for the jay they'd have let him ride by and drilled him in the back. He hated backshooters almost as much as madams who set him up to be backshot.

The pair wore homespun and carried single-shot rifles. They looked more like husbands on a hunt for game rather than hired shootists.

Slowly thumbing back the hammer to mute the click, Fargo centered the front bead and held his breath to steady his aim.

The men had stopped and were looking around, trying to spot him. As assassins went, they were amateurs.

Fargo fired dead center at the man on the right, shifted on his elbows, and sent a slug into the man on the left. Both crumpled. The man on the right lay still, but the man on the left crawled behind a tree. Or most of him did. The lower half of a leg poked out. Fargo aimed at the knee and stroked the trigger. The leg jerked and thrashed and stopped moving.

Fargo let more time go buy. If they were shamming, they'd give themselves away. When neither figure moved, he grabbed his hat and slid out from under the blue spruce.

Jamming his hat on, he crept toward them.

His shot had cored the first man's heart and burst out the back near the spine. The man's head lay with a lifeless eye fixed on the vault of sky.

Fargo moved toward the other one. The leg still hadn't moved. He assumed the killer was dead and stepped around the tree, straight into the muzzle of the man's rifle.

"I've got you, you son of a bitch."

Fargo became stone.

"Frank's dead, ain't he?" the man said. "And you've almost done for me." He coughed violently. Blood trickled from his mouth, and he licked some of it off his lips. "Any last words, you murderous bastard?"

"Me?" Fargo found his voice.

"We told them no, so they hired themselves a gun hand," the man said. "They knew we'd do whatever it took to protect our families and our homes and our town."

"I'm not a killer," Fargo said.

"Tell that to Frank," the man snarled. "Don't act innocent, mister. They bragged on you, you know. On how deadly you are." He showed his blood-smeared teeth in a vicious grin. "This is where I send you to hell."

10

Fargo stared death in the face. He would be shot before he could level the Henry. He looked into the muzzle of the man's rifle, and his skin prickled as he imagined the slug ripping through his brain.

A gun boomed, but not the rifle. There was the *thwack* of lead striking flesh, and the man cried out and his arms dipped.

Gripping the barrel, Fargo wrenched the rifle free. He cast it aside, stepped back, and pointed the Henry while searching for the source of his salvation.

Out of the trees stepped Chester Leghorny, smoke curling from his pistol. He was staring at the man he'd shot as if he couldn't believe he'd shot him.

"Where did you come from?" Fargo said.

Chester blinked and his throat bobbed. "I've been watchin' over you. . . ." he said, and stopped. "I saw you ride off and followed you and . . ." He stared aghast at the assassin. "I ain't ever shot anybody before."

"I'm obliged," Fargo said. "You saved my bacon."

"I did?" Chester did more blinking and looked at him and smiled. "I reckon so, pard."

Fargo was about to tell him to stop calling him that and changed his mind. After this, Chester deserved to call him anything he wanted.

The man on the ground was making gulping sounds and opening and closing his fists. "You . . ." he gasped. "You . . ." He couldn't finish.

Squatting, Fargo said, "Listen to me, mister. I don't know who you think I am—"

"Fargo," the man got out. "Skye Fargo."

"That's right," Fargo said. "I scout for a living. That's no reason to kill me."

"You're more than a scout," the man croaked. "We've heard of you. Heard you've shot a lot of folks."

"Hell," Fargo said. Yes, he'd been in more than his share of scrapes, but he didn't live by the gun as some did. He didn't hire his Colt out. Once or twice he'd done some bounty work, but that was different, and he never liked it much. "The West is full of gents who've shot folks."

"That includes me now," Chester said, and chuckled. "Gosh Almighty. A few more times and people will think *I'm* a gun hand."

"Never in a million years," Fargo said. "Now hush." He leaned over the dying killer. "Who are you? Who hired you to come after me?"

"No one," the man said weakly. "I came after you my own self. To protect my family. My home."

"What in hell are you talking about?" Fargo said. "I'm guiding some wagons from Lodestone to Silver Creek. I'm not out to hurt anyone."

"They are."

"Who?" Fargo said, but knew the answer even as he asked. A chill seemed to run through him.

"That woman and that mayor and those others," the man said, and took a deep breath. "They aim to take us over—lock, stock, and barrel."

"How do you know?" Fargo asked.

"One of them has kin in Silver Creek," the man said, and coughed. "Told us . . . about you."

"Told you what?"

The man was finding it hard to talk. "How that mayor and that woman had heard about you. Heard you were . . . the toughest hombre anywhere."

"You are?" Chester interrupted, looking at Fargo in awe. "I should have guessed. When you gunned Hardy and Wilson so slick, I should have known right then."

"What else?" Fargo said to the man at his feet.

"We took a vote. Decided to . . ." The man stiffened, and his eyes widened, and he said, "Martha! Oh, Martha!" Taking a last breath, he exhaled and was gone.

"Who the blazes is Martha? His horse, you think?" Chester said.

Fargo was mulling the implications of what he'd just heard. The more he learned, the madder he became.

Chester stared at the six-shooter in his hand. "I've done killed a man. Do you know what that means?"

Fargo didn't answer.

"It means I'm a gun hand now. Chester Leghorny, gunman. Has a ring to it, don't you think?"

Fargo forced himself to focus. "It has no ring at all. You're not, and never will be, a gun hand."

"What a mean thing to say, pard," Chester said. "Just think. Once word gets out, I won't have to kowtow to anyone anymore. Bullies will leave me be. When I walk down the street, people will get out of my way."

"Chester . . ." Fargo said.

"I'll be treated with respect for the first time in my life."

"Fear isn't the same as respect."

"It's as close as I'll ever come." Chester hefted his revolver and chuckled. "My pa always said I'd never amount to much, but he was wrong. Why, I bet I could make a livin' at this."

"At shooting people?"

Chester nodded. "I shoot a few more and get the hang of it, I can hire my gun out. Be what they call down Texas way a *pistolero*."

"You shoot anyone else and we're quits," Fargo said. He thought that was a clever way to nip Chester's new dream in the bud.

"Then we *are* pards!" Chester exclaimed. "I knew it. I knew you were just joshin' me."

Fargo let it be for now. "Lend me a hand with these bodies." Shallow graves would do. Ordinarily, he'd have left assassins to rot. But these were family men protecting their own.

"Sure thing, pard," Chester said. "But if you don't mind my sayin', it's a lot of bother to go to for two fellas who tried to shoot you."

"They thought they were doing the right thing."

"I never have known what that was. My ma used to say it's because I'm too dumb to know right from wrong."

"She said that and your pa said you were worthless? Those were some parents you had."

Chester shrugged. "They weren't so bad. Pa only beat me once or twice a week and Ma made tasty flapjacks. I was their only kid. They didn't want any but somehow I came. Ma said I was a curse."

"Did you tell her to go to hell?"

"My own ma?" Chester said, shocked. "Who talks to their mother like that? No, I figured she knew best."

"Let's get to burying," Fargo said more gruffly than he intended. They found downed branches with sharp enough ends and set to scooping dirt for the graves.

56

"Mind if I ask you somethin', pard?" Chester said as they worked. Fargo grunted.

"I've been tryin' to figure this out. Remember that big gal sayin' how she'd painted a target on your back?"

"I'm not about to forget it."

"Is this what she meant?" Chester asked, nodding at the bodies. "That folks would be poppin' up all over the place to do you in?"

"Seems to be," Fargo said.

"But why you? Why not just hire themselves a passel of curly wolves to ride into Silver Creek and clean it out?"

"That would bring the law down on their heads."

"Not if no one knew they'd hired the curly wolves," Chester said. "It seems to me there's somethin' I'm missin' here. There must be more to it."

"Could be," Fargo said, "and if so, I'll find out."

"How?"

"By playing along for the time being."

"That could get you dead. But don't worry. I'll be watchin' your back every minute. Anyone tries to put lead into you, they'll do it over my dead body."

"I don't need a nursemaid."

"I'm not," Chester said, grinning happily. "I'm your pard."

Fargo bent and gouged the branch into the soil. Like it or not, for a while at least, it seemed he was stuck with one.

Before they rolled the bodies into the holes, Fargo went through each man's pockets. He found a few coins and part of a plug of tobacco and that was all. No wads of money, like the others. Nothing to say who they were.

"I'm glad that's over with," Chester said once the mounds of dirt were tamped down.

Fargo was thinking of the time. They'd spent almost an hour at it, and the wagon train must have been getting close. "Make yourself scarce. The crowd from Lodestone will be here any minute."

"Remember," Chester said as he walked off, "I'll be watchin' your back."

Wondering how it was he got into these situations, Fargo reclaimed the Ovaro and rode to the road. No sooner did he emerge from the trees than he heard the creak and rattle of approaching wagons. He stayed where he was, leaning on the saddle horn, and soon the first Conestoga rolled into view. The man driving hollered something, and Mayor Quilby and Arthur Thomas rode up the line.

"Here you are," the mayor said as he drew rein. "We were worried. You've been gone quite a while."

"We thought we heard shots earlier," Arthur Thomas said.

"Shots?" Fargo shammed ignorance.

"There have already been attempts on your life," Mayor Quilby said, as if Fargo needed reminding.

"We wouldn't want anything to happen to you," the treasurer threw in.

For two bits Fargo would have slugged him. "I've been wondering about something."

"Such as?" Mayor Quilby said.

"How many folks live in Silver Creek?"

"What does their population have to do with anything?" Quilby asked suspiciously.

"I'd estimate they have a couple of hundred," Arthur Thomas said. "About half work in the mine. The rest run businesses and the like."

"That's a sizable boomtown," Fargo said.

"Sizable enough," Mayor Quilby said. "It could be a lot bigger if the right folks were in charge."

"Would you be one of them?"

"Why not?" Quilby said. "I can run for public office there the same as I can anywhere else."

"There's a lot that could improve Silver Creek," Arthur Thomas said. "Their very own sporting house, for instance."

"Run by Gladiola Thimblebottom," Fargo said.

Quilby smiled. "It's what she does. The one she ran in Lodestone was a model of efficiency. You wouldn't think it to look at her, but Gladiola has an exceptional head on her shoulders."

"The salt of the earth, that woman," Arthur Thomas said.

Fargo was tired of being played for a fool. "Call a halt and we'll rest for half an hour."

"So soon?" Mayor Quilby said.

"We won't need to rest until sundown," Arthur Thomas said.

"Call a halt anyway."

Puzzled, the mayor and the treasurer nonetheless did as Fargo requested. The wagons were brought to a stop and the drivers climbed down to stretch their legs.

Fargo rode along the train until he came to Gladiola Thimblebottom's Conestoga. She was nowhere around, but Hortense had knelt and was examining a front wheel. "It's been squeaking a lot," she said as he dismounted.

"Might need some axle grease. Has the wheel wobbled any?"

"Not that I'm aware," Hortense said.

"Then it sounds like it can wait until we stop for the night." Fargo helped her to her feet, and she pressed against him, smiling playfully.

"I've been thinking of you all morning. Your stunt in the hallway made me hungry for more."

"You've changed your mind about tonight?"

Hortense glanced up and down the train. "I'm thinking about it. But we dare not let Gladiola find out."

"Find out what?" the female mountain said, and came around the horses. She had put a bonnet on and was carrying a handbag. Most women, it would make them seem more feminine. On her, it was as if a cow buffalo decided to playact.

"Nothing," Hortense said.

Fargo turned. "She doesn't want you to know that we're sneaking off tonight after everyone has turned in."

"Only if you say it's all right," Hortense said, giving Fargo an annoyed look.

"It's not," Gladiola said. "Save your fooling around for town. Out here too many things can happen."

"Like what?" Fargo said.

"Oh, you know," Gladiola said, and her great rounded shoulders rose up and down.

"She'll be with me. Nothing will happen to her."

"You forget that Hortense works for me," Gladiola said. "I say whether she does or she doesn't and tonight she doesn't."

"You're awful bossy," Fargo said. "Must come from being the world's biggest bitch."

Gladiola's moon face drained of color. "What did you just say to me?"

"Can't you hear with that bonnet over your ears?"

"Yes," Gladiola said. "They work right fine."

And then she hit him.

11

Fargo had been trying to get her goat. To rile her a little to get back at her for her part in their scheme to use him. He figured she'd get mad. He never thought she'd attack him.

Gladiola Thimblebottom was strong. The punch rocked him on his bootheels and into Hortense, who stumbled and grabbed the front wheel to keep from falling.

"Gladiola, no!" Hortense cried.

Fargo shook off the blow and rubbed his chin. "Not bad," he said.

Livid, Gladiola boasted, "I've licked men twice your size."

"With your fists or your tongue?"

"You'd better stop," Gladiola warned.

"Or what? You'll sit on me and crush me?"

"Skye, please don't," Hortense pleaded. "Why are you doing this? We're on the same side here, aren't we?"

"What I want to know," Fargo said, not taking his eyes off Gladiola, "is whether you were a man right out of the womb, or whether you had to work at it."

"Oh, Skye," Hortense said.

Gladiola Thimblebottom gripped the strap to her handbag in both hands. "That was your last insult."

Fargo put his hands on his hips. "Lady, I'm just warming up. You made a mistake when you picked me to take part in your grand scheme. You can go to hell and take Quilby with you."

"You first," Gladiola said, and swung.

Fargo sidestepped. That she was attacking him with her bag was just plain silly. He avoided her first swing but wasn't quite quick enough to dodge the next. Her handbag caught him across the chin.

It was like running into a boulder. His head burst with pain, and his vision swam, and his knees threatened to buckle. Gamely, he staggered back and swiped at his eyes, trying to clear them.

"What's the matter, tough guy?" Gladiola said. "You can't take being hit by a purse?"

Fargo backed out of reach. Whatever she had in that thing mustn't connect a second time. She came at him swinging, and he ducked. Scowling, Gladiola came after him, her eyes blazing.

"Gladiola, what are you doing?" Hortense cried.

"Shut up, whore," Gladiola snarled. "You heard him. He has this coming. Anyone tries to stop me, I'll do the same to them."

Fargo set himself. He'd taken all he was going to.

"You think you can insult folks," Gladiola said. "Act like you're better than us when you're not."

"Says the cow who thinks she's a bull."

Gladiola planted her tree-trunk legs and cocked her arms. "I'll tell you a secret. I like walloping men. I like to beat them senseless and stomp on their faces and kick them in their manly parts."

"You're just jealous you don't have any."

That did it. Gladiola howled like an enraged wolf and swept at him in a rush, swinging her handbag as if it were a club.

This time, Fargo was ready. He tucked his legs, and the bag knocked his hat from his head. In retaliation, he unleashed an uppercut and smashed her full on her jaw. That should have been enough. Most men would have been down, either unconscious or in agony.

Not Gladiola Thimblebottom. She took a half step back, moved her chin from side to side, and said, "Is that the best you've got?"

"Hell," Fargo said, genuinely amazed.

"Great scout, my ass," Gladiola said. "You're downright puny."

Fargo looked at his fist. He'd hit her with nearly all he had.

"You see, Hortense?" Gladiola said. "Men aren't so much. They strut and put on airs but they're nothing. They're not good for anything except to have babies."

"That's not true," Hortense said. "Some of them are sweet and kind."

"Not this one," Gladiola said, nodding at Fargo. "He's snake mean, but he hides it real well."

"When men fight," Fargo said, "they don't gab each other to death."

Gladiola firmed her grip on the strap. "Men!" she spat. "Always insulting women for being women."

"No," Fargo said. "I'm insulting you because you're a bitch. I thought I'd made that plain?"

Gladiola lost her self-control. Uttering a shriek of rage, she flew at him like an avalanche.

Fargo twisted and took her swing on the shoulder. It hurt, but not nearly as much as her next, which caught him across the ribs.

She was quick for her size. He wouldn't have suspected it. He got his left arm up and blocked another blow, and his forearm flared with torment. Suddenly lunging, he got hold of the handbag and sought to wrench it from her grasp. Gladiola clung on. Hissing, she slammed her hip against his. He nearly went down. Holding on, he spun, seeking to unbalance and trip her. She took a short step, recovered, and kicked him in the leg. She'd gone for his knee and caught the top of his shin. His leg partially buckled but he stayed on his feet. He pulled on her bag but couldn't tear it from her. Instead, she tore it loose and took a step back, smiling smugly.

People were gathering. Voices murmured. Mayor Quilby exclaimed, "What on earth is going on here?"

"Someone stop them," Arthur Thomas said.

"Not me," someone said. "I don't want Gladiola mad at me."

Gladiola smiled. She ate up their fear with a spoon. "Time to end this," she announced, and waded in again.

Fargo realized she had backed him close to the trees. As she advanced, he slipped around a sapling, putting it between them. "Come and get me, cow."

"See if I don't," Gladiola said. Her huge arms pumped and her bag thudded against the sapling.

Fargo grabbed a strap. He hauled backward but he might as well have tried to move a glacier. She braced herself and wouldn't be moved. Acting on sudden inspiration, he pulled harder. Gladiola grinned. He dug his heels in and threw every sinew into seeking to pull her off-balance. Or so he wanted her to think.

Gladiola laughed and glanced at Hortense. "Look at him. I can whip him with one hand tied behind my back."

"Whip this," Fargo said, and let go.

His strategy worked. Gladiola was taken off guard and tottered. She tried to right herself, failed, and fell against a horse. The animal shied but couldn't go anywhere and threw itself against her. The upshot was that Gladiola pitched heavily to her hands and knees.

Some of the onlookers cackled.

A couple of steps and Fargo was above her, cocking his arm. It was oh so tempting.

"Skye," Hortense cried, "don't!"

"That will be enough," Mayor Quilby said. "Are we adults or are we children here?"

"Ask the grizzly in the dress," Fargo said.

Gladiola rammed into him. Fargo swiveled but couldn't avoid

her. She swept his legs out from under him, and the next he knew, he was on his back.

Gladiola hurled her bulk on top of him. "I have you right where I want you, you son of a bitch."

Fargo couldn't believe it. He was being whipped by a woman. She grabbed for his wrists to pin him even as she drove her leg between his, going for his groin. He managed to shift and took her dirty trick on his thigh. Whipping his right arm up, he slugged her.

The only effect it had was to make her blink. Then, growling like the bear she resembled, Gladiola raised her head high and swept her forehead at his face. Fargo twisted and the side of his head burst with new pain. He punched her and pressed his forearm to her thick neck to keep her from head-butting him again.

People were yelling for someone to stop the fight but no one apparently dared. Hortense cried Gladiola's name over and over.

Gladiola gouged her fingers into Fargo's throat. Her dark eyes glittering with pure hate, she squeezed and said, "I'm going to throttle you."

Fargo drew his fist as far back as it would go and drove it against her temple. He didn't expect it to do much. So far nothing he had done seemed to hurt her. To his surprise, though, her eyelids fluttered and her grip weakened, and just like that, she collapsed on top of him.

Fargo gasped for breath. It felt as if he were being crushed. He pushed but she was too heavy.

Mayor Quilby barked commands. Hands appeared, a lot of them, and Gladiola was eased off and rolled onto her back.

Fargo slowly made it to his feet. He hurt all over. As if he'd been in a barroom brawl with four or five men. He rubbed his throat and looked at Gladiola. No wonder people were afraid of her.

"God Almighty," a man said. "That was some fight, mister."

Mouse was there and remarked, "How did you do so good against me? She's a girl, and she about walloped you."

Fargo was tempted to say that Gladiola was a lot tougher, but he didn't need another fight.

"What set her off, anyhow?" Mayor Quilby asked.

"Beats me," Fargo said.

Hortense looked sharply at him but held her tongue.

"I'd advise you to make yourself scarce for a while," Quilby suggested. "When we revive her, she's liable to be so mad, she'll come after you again."

"I've never seen a female like her before," Arthur Thomas said. "She'll tangle with any man, anytime."

"Good for her," a woman said.

Fargo decided to take the mayor's advice. He'd be damned if he'd let Thimblebottom tear into him again. The next time he wouldn't hold back.

Picking up his hat, he dusted it off and jammed it on, and winced.

Hortense came over to whisper, "I tried to warn you not to rile her. Why didn't you listen?"

"I don't like having a target on my back."

"How do you mean?"

Fargo realized she wasn't in on the deception. Evidently only Lodestone's civic leaders were a party to it. "Never mind," he said. "See you later." Making sure his Colt was in his holster, he strode off.

When he forked leather, he grimaced. His legs were sore from where Gladiola kicked him and tried to knee him.

Heading up the road, Fargo put her from his mind. He had a bigger worry. The people of Silver Creek were still out to perforate him. He watched the woods on both sides and hadn't gone far when a rider appeared amid the trees. He swooped his hand to his Colt but didn't draw.

Chester Leghorny reached the road and felt in alongside the Ovaro. "I'm plumb embarrassed, pard," he announced.

"What do you have to be embarrassed about?" Fargo asked.

"You."

"This should be good," Fargo said.

"I saw the whole thing. You were almost whipped by a female. My own pard. If that's not embarrassin', I don't know what is."

"In the first place, she's a hill on legs. In the second, anytime you reckon you can do better, walk up to her and call her a bitch."

"Females are puny," Chester said. "Everybody knows that."

"Everybody is wrong."

"I'm still embarrassed. I almost ran out to help you. If she'd killed you, where would that leave me?"

"Alive."

"Be serious. I'd still be breathin', but where would I go? What would I do? I sure couldn't go around tellin' everybody I lost my pard when he was stomped by a petticoat. I'd be a laughingstock."

"You have a hard life," Fargo said.

"Ain't that the truth. Then again, she is sort of scary. She sure scared me when she came to the jail."

64

Fargo almost drew rein. "She did what?"

"Back in Lodestone. After you threw me in that cell. She shocked the bejabbers out of me by waddlin' on in."

"How is it you never mentioned this before?"

Chester shrugged. "I didn't think much of it at the time. I figured she was lookin' for you or that mayor. She came over to the bars and studied on me, and then she said, 'You sure are an ugly little runt.'"

"What did you do?"

Chester flicked his hand at a fly that was buzzing him. "I was sort of flabbergasted, her talkin' to me like that. But I told her she was a fine one to talk about ugly."

"How did she take that?"

"About how you'd expect. She sneered at me and said, 'Men.' Then she said somethin' that I thought was strange and stomped out like a mad bull. Or bein' as she's female, a mad heifer."

"Strange how?"

"She said that I wouldn't be the last person to try and take your life. There would be a whole passel out to get you. And then she laughed." Chester rubbed his chin. "She's some gal, huh?"

"Some gal," Fargo said.

12

Crossing the Divide was spectacular. A sweeping vista of pristine peaks and verdant forest stretched to the western horizon. The sun, well on its downward arc, painted the sky with vivid hues of pink and orange.

Mayor Quilby wanted to stop so everyone could admire the view.

Fargo said no. The spot where he wanted to make camp was a mile below and they would be lucky to get there before night fell.

"It's a shame," Quilby said. "Moments like these, you want to pause and give thanks to the Almighty for being alive."

"I'm happy to be," Fargo said.

"You must be referring to your many skirmishes with savages and the like," Quilby said.

Fargo couldn't resist baiting him with, "At least with Indians, you usually know when they're on the warpath."

Their descent went slowly. The slopes were steep, and the drivers held their teams to a cautious walk.

Twice, Fargo went back up the line and each time got a warm smile from Hortense.

From Gladiola Thimblebottom all he got were glares. She sat on the seat with Hortense, her eyes pits of molten fire.

They arrived at the campsite as the last sliver of sun faded. Travelers often used it. Blackened coals marked where fires were kindled. A gurgling stream provided water.

Once the Conestogas were in a circle and supper was being cooked, Fargo was left to himself. He made his own little fire and put coffee on to brew. He dragged a log over for a seat and had been sitting there a while when the mayor and the mayor's shadow, the treasurer, approached.

"I wanted to tell you how pleased we are," Quilby said. "We're making excellent time."

"There haven't been any problems at all," Arthur Thomas said. "Well, not counting that fracas you had with Gladiola."

Fargo hadn't told anyone about his scrape with the men from Silver Creek. "She hasn't said a word to me since."

"Nor to anyone else," Mayor Quilby said. "I asked Hortense and she told me that Gladiola won't even talk to her."

"Gladiola is just mad," Arthur Thomas said.

"I hope that's all it is." Quilby said. "She's unpredictable, that woman."

"Was it her idea or yours to move to Silver Creek?" Fargo fished for information.

"I don't know as I remember," Quilby said.

"I do," Arthur Thomas said. "Gladiola came up with it. At that town meeting when everyone was wringing their hands over what to do when the gold played out. I've got to say, that woman has a head on her shoulders."

"The people in Silver Creek might not think so."

Quilby said testily, "It's not as if we need their permission. This is a free country. A man or woman can move where they please. They'd have no legal ground to stand on if they tried to stop us."

"That's right," Arthur Thomas said.

"Do you think they will?" Fargo played the innocent.

"Who can tell with people?" Quilby said. "They get notions into their heads and do all kinds of things." He nudged Thomas. "Let's go see about the others. And then we can relax for a while."

Fargo wished he could. There was enough light in the circle that an assassin in the woods could easily pick him off. He touched his coffeepot, but it wasn't hot enough yet.

Perfume wreathed him, and Hortense came around and gracefully eased down. "Hope you don't mind a visit?"

"I'm surprised she'd let you," Fargo said.

Hortense colored. "She doesn't control me, I'll have you know."

"You work for her."

"And that's the only capacity in which she has a say," Hortense said. "Who I sleep with when I'm not working is none of her affair." She smiled and winked. "You should know that by now."

"When does she plan to stab me in the back?"

Hortense laughed without much merriment. "Think what you will of her, she's not as despicable as that. She'll come at you head-on like she did today."

"Good to know," Fargo said.

"You're just lucky she didn't shoot you. She carries a revolver in her handbag."

Fargo remembered the heavy object that had about split his skull. "So that's what it was." He made a show of admiring her figure. "Do I come fetch you once everyone has turned in?"

"I told you before," Hortense said, "I'm not sure it's wise. Gladiola will throw a fit if she finds out."

"You're worth the risk," Fargo flattered her.

"I don't know," Hortense said uncertainly, but there was a hint of desire in her tone. "I'd like to. I honestly would."

"Are you sleeping in the wagon or out of it?"

"There's no room inside to sleep," Hortense said. "It's filled with the furniture and whatnot for Gladiola's new Passion Palace."

"Her what?"

"That's what she's thinking of calling it. We'll be sleeping outside, next to the wagon. Don't let her hear you."

"I'll hoot like an owl, and you sneak over to me."

"An owl?" Hortense said, and sniggered.

"I could imitate a raven, but they don't usually squawk at night."

"An owl is fine." Hortense stood and smoothed her dress. "I can't believe you've talked me into it."

"Didn't take much talking," Fargo said.

67

Hortense started to go but stopped and placed her hand on his shoulder. "If it was up to me, I'd take you into the woods and ride you until we died of starvation."

"Not me," Fargo said. "I'd have plenty to eat."

"I didn't say I'd bring food."

"Me either."

Hortense laughed uproariously, caught herself, and covered her mouth with her hand. "You're so naughty. It excites me to no end."

"You'll have a chance to prove that later," Fargo said.

"See if I don't," Hortense said, and playfully flicked her fingernail across his cheek.

Fargo watched her sashay away. He checked his coffee again. By now it was hot. Filling his tin cup, he sat and sipped and pondered the day's events. He figured everyone would leave him alone but he was wrong.

A shadow fell over him and a dress rustled and Gladiola Thimblebottom loomed out of the night. She was carrying her handbag but made no attempt to resort to her hardware. "We need to talk."

"News to me," Fargo said.

"It was wrong for me to lay into you like I did," Gladiola said. "If I can't take a little name-calling, I don't deserve to be in the business I'm in."

Not for a second did Fargo think she was sincere. "I might have stepped over the line."

"No might about it. Calling someone a bitch isn't a compliment." Gladiola balled her fists but relaxed them again. "Enough about that. I'm willing to start over if you are."

"Meaning?"

"I'll be nice if you'll be nice."

Fargo made a show of scanning the ground around them.

"What are you doing?"

"Waiting for the earth to open up and swallow me."

Gladiola wasn't amused. "I come here to make peace, and you throw it in my face. So much for Quilby's bright idea." She turned to go.

"This was the mayor's doing?"

"He's worried you'll quit on us," Gladiola said, "so he begged me to come apologize. Me, I'd just as soon kick you in the nuts."

"That's the Gladiola I know and love," Fargo said.

"Go to hell." She rounded on him and jabbed a finger. "I don't like you. Not a little bit. You're everything I thought you'd be when we sent for you."

"Then why did you?" Fargo asked.

"Because we needed someone like you," Gladiola replied. "Some-one they would—" She stopped.

"They?"

"These other folks," Gladiola said, with a sweep of her arm at those in the circle, "they needed someone they would trust to get them to Silver Creek."

Fargo had to hand it to her. She could lie as glibly as anyone.

Gladiola wasn't done. "You taught me a lesson today and I should thank you for that. I went easy on you and I shouldn't have. The next time you insult me, I will by-God bury you." She curled her lips in a fake sweet smile and stalked off.

"This is some wagon train," Fargo said.

Most everyone turned in early. It had been a long day and tomor-row they had almost as many hours to travel. Some folks might think that riding on a wagon seat wasn't tiring but handling a large wagon on steep slopes frayed the nerves and the muscles.

By eleven or so only two men were still up, talking. It was push-ing midnight when they finally stopped swapping tales and made for their bedrolls.

Fargo glanced over at where Hortense and Gladiola were sleep-ing. Or appeared to be. He waited another ten minutes, then stood and crooked the Henry in his arm and walked slowly about as if he were stretching his legs. His meandering took him close to Hortense. He wanted to get her attention but she was on her side, her face covered by her blanket.

Gladiola was on her back. Her mouth was open and she was snoring.

Fargo gave the circle a quick scrutiny, then went between Hortense's Conestoga and the next and stepped over the tongue into darkness. Standing where he could see her, he cupped his hand to his mouth and softly hooted. He'd heard enough owls in his travels that he sounded like the real article.

Hortense didn't move.

Fargo tried again, a little louder. Gladiola stopped snoring and he swore under his breath, thinking he had woken her. After a bit her snoring resumed.

Hortense still showed no sign that she was awake.

Squatting, Fargo groped about until he found a pebble. Then, taking great care, he threw it so it hit Hortense in the back.

Nothing happened.

"Damn it to hell," Fargo groused. He was looking forward to

doing her again. A second pebble proved harder to find. He threw it just as carefully and it struck her on the shoulder.

Hortense just lay there.

"Damn it." Fargo stepped over the tongue and walked up to her and shook her shoulder. Hortense gave a start and rolled over and opened her mouth. Quickly, he clamped his hand over it and whispered in her ear, "Not a sound."

Hortense glanced at Gladiola and nodded.

Letting go, Fargo pulled her blanket down, offered her his hand, and pulled her to her feet.

"I thought you were going to hoot like an owl?" she whispered.

"I must have forgot." Fargo made for the gap, never once taking his eyes off Thimblebottom.

Hortense suddenly tugged on his shirt and pointed.

Across the way, a sleeper had sat up and was yawning and scratching himself. For a moment Fargo thought the man would turn in their direction but he lay back down, smacked his lips, and was still.

"That was close," Hortense whispered. "I know him. He'd tell Gladiola if he saw us sneaking off."

Fargo helped her over the tongue and steered her into the woods. She pressed against him, out of desire, he thought, but he was mistaken.

"It's spooky out here at night. Aren't you afraid?"

"Of the dark? I'm not ten years old anymore."

"Of the things that come out at night," Hortense said. "The grizzlies and the big cats, and the ghosts."

Fargo snorted.

"You don't believe that people come back from the dead to haunt us?"

"You do?"

"We had a ghost in the farmhouse where I grew up. My ma said it was the ghost of her ma, come to watch over us."

"Uh-huh."

"I saw it myself, twice. A shimmering light in the shape of a person. It about scared me to death."

"How much did you have to drink?"

"Don't scoff, damn you. I was a little girl at the time. The first time, I bawled my brains out and it took my mother—" Hortense abruptly stopped. Not just talking, but walking, too.

"What's the matter?" Fargo said.

Hortense looked pale and the whites of her eyes were showing. "Here we are talking about them and there one is."

"There what is?" Fargo asked in annoyance.

"A ghost," Hortense said, and pointed.

13

Fargo looked.

Off through the trees a light flickered and swayed. At first glance it could have been mistaken for something otherworldly, but Fargo knew better. "It's a torch." Even as he said it, a second and a third light appeared.

"Who can it be at this time of night?" Hortense said. "Indians?"

Fargo doubted it. Indians had more sense than to traipse around in a forest at night. Whoever it was, they were west of the camp. How far was hard to say. The torches were spaced well apart, each casting a circle of light dappled by shadows.

Taking Hortense's hand, he said, "Quick. Let's go back."

"Do you know who they are?"

"Not yet." But Fargo did have a suspicion. He pulled on her arm to make her move faster.

"Well, darn. Now our fun will have to wait. What a shame."

Fargo hurried her into the circle. Letting go, he ran to where Mayor Quilby lay sound asleep and drooling. He poked Quilby with a toe, and when that didn't work, he kicked him.

"What in the world?" the mayor sputtered, sitting up and looking about in confusion.

"Get everyone up as quietly as you can," Fargo said. "Arm the men and put out the fires."

"What? Why?"

"Just do it."

Arthur Thomas sat up, saying, "What's going on? What's going on?"

Fargo ran to the wagons on the west wide of the clearing and climbed onto a seat. From his perch he saw not three but half a dozen torches, steadily advancing.

A townsman came up, sleepily rubbing his eyes. "What are you doing on my wagon?"

"We have company coming. If you have a rifle, get it and join the rest," Fargo advised. Thankfully, the man didn't pester him with more questions. He gauged that it would be five minutes or more before the men holding the torches got there. Time he could use to good advantage.

Hopping down, Fargo hurried to where the mayor and Arthur Thomas were waking sleepers. "Company is coming. I'm going to go see who it is."

"The Utes?" Quilby said in blatant fear.

"No. Once everyone is up and armed, have them take cover behind the wagons."

"You think whoever is out there will attack us?"

"They're not coming to invite us to a square dance." Fargo turned and bounded out of the circle and into the woods. Moving swiftly toward the torches, he couldn't avoid the occasional crunch of a leaf or the rustle of a bush that snagged his buckskins.

When he had gone approximately two hundred yards, Fargo hunkered behind a tree. It was far enough. He could see the men holding the torches. They were white, and they all had rifles. Others were with them. Twenty or more, Fargo reckoned. But where soldiers would know not to make a peep, these were talking back and forth.

"How much farther?"

"We're almost there."

"What happened to their fires? I saw a couple but now I don't."

"It's late. The fires must have burned themselves out."

Fargo let them get close enough that he could drop a few if he had to and called out, "That's far enough."

They stopped in their tracks, the men with the torches raising them higher so the light spread farther into the trees.

"Who's there?" demanded a man in the middle. He wore a suit and a derby, and a gold watch chain gleamed in his vest. In the torchlight his mustache looked gray. In addition to a rifle, he had a six-shooter around his waist.

"You first," Fargo said.

"I'm Mayor Artemis Pike."

"From Silver Creek?" Fargo guessed.

72

"Is there any other town in these parts?" Pike replied. "These men with me are also residents of our fair community."

Only a politician, Fargo reflected, would talk that like. "It's a little late for a stroll in the woods."

"You haven't told us who you are," Mayor Pike said.

Fargo did.

Immediately a man exclaimed, "It's him! The killer they hired."

"So what?" another said. "He can't stop all of us. We're too many."

"Gentlemen, please," Mayor Pike said. "Silence, if you would." He peered in Fargo's direction. "We've heard of you, mister."

"I'm not a hired killer," Fargo set him straight. "I scout for a living."

"Some scout," Mayor Pike said. "Seven men were sent to dispose of you and not one has returned."

"*You* sent them?"

"It would be foolish of me to admit, wouldn't it, given that it's illegal to pay to have someone killed? But I will say that the last two came on their own. I tried to persuade them not to but they had a strong sense of civic duty."

"Killing me is a duty?"

"When you are part and parcel of the pernicious scheme to ruin the town all of us hold so dear, yes."

"I'm not out to ruin anything," Fargo said. "All I'm doing is leading the people of Lodestone to Silver Creek to live."

"It's the same thing," Mayor Pike said.

A figure on his right snapped, "Why are we listening to this hombre? Let's rush him. With the scout out of the way, the rest will be easy."

"Patience, Charles," Mayor Pike said. He raised his voice, "Fargo, what did that pathetic wretch and vile woman tell you their plans are?"

"By wretch, you must mean Quilby and by vile woman you must mean Gladiola Thimblebottom."

"The very two."

"They told me they want to move to Silver Creek."

"That's all? No mention of their intent beyond that?"

"Thimblebottom wants to open a sporting house."

"Over our dead bodies," Mayor Pike said. "In case they haven't told you, the people of our community are devoted to good, clean living. The men who work in our mine and run our shops are mostly family men. They like a law-abiding town where they can live in peace."

"That we do, mister," a man hollered.

"Your friends," Mayor Pike began, then said, "or, rather, those who hired you, want to change all that. The woman would bring her whores, and Quilby would turn Silver Creek into the same pit of vice and corruption that Lodestone was before their ore played out. We won't allow that."

"We sure as hell won't!" another man shouted.

"We were informed when they sent for you," Mayor Pike said. "I was unfamiliar with who you are, so I asked around and found that you have a reputation for being 'a formidable man to tangle with,' was how one acquaintance phrased it."

"We'll by-God tangle with you," someone said, and several laughed.

"You could have come talk to me," Fargo said. "Instead you hired gun hands."

"Our homes and are families are at stake," Mayor Pike echoed the sentiments of the townsman Fargo had clashed with earlier in the day.

"Why are you here?"

"That should be obvious," Mayor Pike said. "Our previous attempts to stop you—and them—have failed. So we're taking matters into our own hands." He gazed along the skirmish line. "I'd hoped that at this late hour, all of you would be asleep. We'd hoped to approach undetected, disarm you, and send you back over the Divide."

"Is your law dog with you?" Fargo was curious to learn.

"Marshal Sadler is not," Mayor Pike said. "He doesn't agree with our methods. But he had the decency not to try to stop us."

"They're ready for you," Fargo said. "Turn around and go home before it's too late."

"Haven't you been paying attention?" Mayor Pike said. "It's already too late. We warned Quilby and Thimblebottom and their minions not to come. I personally sent a rider with a letter to that scoundrel stating in no uncertain terms that he and his ilk aren't welcome in Silver Creek. Do you know what he did?" Pike didn't wait for an answer. "He tore my letter up and had the rider stick the pieces in his hat and bring them back to me. In effect, he threw my warning in my face."

"What did you do then?"

"Nothing. We waited to hear what they would do, and that's when word came to us that they had sent for you."

Fargo scowled. All the pieces to the puzzle were in place. Now he must decide what to do about it. He'd be damned if he'd do Quilby's fighting for him. Or for any of them.

"Will you give way or must we go through you?" Mayor Pike asked.

Fargo heard gun hammers click.

"Quit wasting your breath," a man demanded. "He must have killed Homer and Dan, and they were our friends."

"Did you, mister?" Mayor Pike said. "Did you kill two men from Silver Creek today?"

"They were trying to kill me," Fargo said.

"There! You heard him!" cried the man who had just spoken. "Shoot the son of a bitch, boys!"

"No! Wait!" Mayor Pike shouted.

No one listened. Rifles boomed in a thunderous volley, their muzzles stabbing flame in the darkness.

Fargo threw himself flat a heartbeat before lead buzzed overhead and to either side. The men from Silver Creek had a fair idea where he was, but they were firing blind and most shot too high. The moment the shooting stopped, he whipped around and crawled until it was safe to rise.

Fargo sprinted for the wagons. Nothing he could do or say would stop the bloodbath. Except possibly one thing.

The fires had been extinguished, and the circle of wagons was dark. "It's Fargo!" he hollered to keep from being shot by mistake.

"Over here!" Mayor Quilby shouted. He was with Arthur Thomas and Gladiola Thimblebottom and some others. "Who's out there and what do they want?"

"It's Mayor Pike and—" Fargo started to say.

"Men from Silver Creek," Mayor Quilby finished. "It's not as if we haven't expected something like this."

"They won't stop us," Arthur Thomas vowed.

"They sure as hell won't," Gladiola Thimblebottom rumbled.

"Is their marshal with them?" Quilby asked.

"They told me he isn't," Fargo said.

"Good," Gladiola said. "They made a mistake coming to confront us. In town, they'd have the law on their side. Here they're no better than a pack of outlaws. We're within our rights to plant every single one."

"I heard about the letter Pike sent you," Fargo said to Quilby. "The one you didn't bother to answer."

"Why should I?" Quilby said. "He warned us to stay away from Silver Creek, or else."

"Who does he think he is?" Gladiola said.

"He's not alone," Fargo said.

"I don't care. Now's as good a time as any to have it come to a head. We'll settle their hash and go on into Silver Creek tomorrow as pretty as you please."

"What if they settle yours?"

"We have enough guns to hold our own," Mayor Quilby said. "Plus we have a surprise we set up while you were out there talking."

Fargo glanced around the clearing. "What sort of surprise?"

"A couple of kegs of black powder," Mayor Quilby revealed. "Off in the trees a safe distance. As soon as those clods from Silver Creek are close enough, we'll set the kegs off."

Gladiola grinned. "It was my idea. The explosions should do a lot of them in. Enough that we can lick the rest."

"A brilliant stroke, my dear," Quilby said. "If you were a man, you'd make a fine general."

"Don't insult me like that," Gladiola said indignantly. "I wouldn't be a man for all the gold in the Rockies."

"Now, now," Quilby said.

"Don't use that tone with me."

Quilby frowned. "Must you always be so prickly?"

"I can see the torches clearly," Arthur Thomas announced.

"They think they're so smart, coming on us late at night," Mayor Quilby said, and laughed.

"We should thank you for keeping them occupied," Arthur Thomas said to Fargo.

Fargo felt little sympathy for the men from Silver Creek. They'd tried to kill him and had brought this on themselves. By the same token, he'd grown to despise those who'd hired him. Taking a step back, he leveled the Henry at Quilby. "I can't let you blow them up."

"What you want doesn't count," Gladiola said, and looked past him. "Mouse, if you would be so kind."

A hard object gouged the back of Fargo's neck.

"This here is a shotgun," Mouse said, "and it'll take your head clean off."

14

Fargo froze except to say, "Go easy with that hand howitzer. I like my head where it is."

Mayor Quilby motioned and two men relieved Fargo of the Henry and his Colt. "We won't let you interfere. Not when we've been given a golden opportunity to get rid of Pike and the others who oppose us."

"Golden," Arthur Thomas said, and snickered.

Gladiola Thimblebottom stepped up to Fargo and poked him in the chest. "Not feeling so high and mighty now, are you?" She poked him again. "I never have liked you, not from the moment I set eyes on you."

"Enough of your rancor," Mayor Quilby said. "We'll deal with him after we've dealt with the Silver Creek crowd."

"Take him away," Gladiola barked at Mouse. "Over to the other side of the clearing where he can't cause mischief. And Mouse?"

"Yes, ma'am?"

"If he gives you a lick of trouble, you let him have it, you hear?"

"Don't worry yourself, ma'am," Mouse said. "I owe him for in town. I'll gladly blow him to hell and back."

Hortense hadn't uttered a word. Now she started to say something but bowed her head as if afraid to.

"You heard the lady," Mouse said. "March."

His hands out from his sides, Fargo turned. He wasn't prepared for a brutal blow to his lower back. Before he could help himself, he was on his hands and knees, awash in torment.

"What did you do that for?" Mayor Quilby angrily asked.

"Because I wanted to," Mouse replied.

"We don't have time for your shenanigans. Pike and his men are almost upon us."

"Leave Mouse be," Gladiola said. "The scout had it coming. Before this is over, I aim to hurt him a lot worse."

"Help Mouse," Quilby said to two others. "Carry Fargo if he can't manage on his own."

The pair seized Fargo's arms and hauled him to his feet. He deliberately let them bear all his weight.

Behind them, Mouse chuckled as if it were a great joke.

Fargo girded himself. The waves of pain were fading, and a furtive glance showed that Mouse was no longer pointing the shotgun at him.

"I reckon this jasper must feel pretty stupid right about now," Mouse said, and the others laughed.

"He'll feel even more stupid when he finds out what Quilby has planned," one of the men remarked.

The second man nodded. "Quilby aims to tell the law that it was Fargo who killed Pike and the rest."

The three of them slowed to look back.

Just then Mayor Quilby shouted, "That's far enough, Pike! Come any closer and we'll open fire."

"We're here to stop you," was the reply from the benighted forest. "By any means necessary."

"You have no right!" Quilby yelled.

"Silver Creek is *our* town. Agree to turn around or there will be hell to pay."

"Let's talk it over," Quilby offered.

Mouse chuckled. "That mayor of ours is a hoot. In another minute he'll blow them to hell."

Quilby had taken a smoldering brand from a fire and was puffing on it. The end glowed red and a tiny flame appeared.

Fargo had moments in which to act. Placing his boots flat, he dragged his heels, causing the men holding him to stumble.

"What the hell?" one blurted, losing his grip.

Wrenching his arm free, Fargo whipped his fist into the face of the second one.

The man staggered. Mouse tried to bring the shotgun to bear but Fargo sidestepped and gripped the barrel in an attempt to wrest it free.

Mouse, swearing, held on. "Get hold of him, damn you!" he shouted at the others. "Don't just stand there."

The pair pounced.

Fargo was a blur. He punched the man on the right in the throat, spun, and struck the second man in the gut. Then, seizing the second man by the shirt, Fargo flung him at Mouse and both went down.

Momentarily in the clear, Fargo flew toward a gap in the wagons. "Shoot him!"

Mouse raised the shotgun. Only now did he thumb back the hammers.

Fargo heard the clicks and dived. The blast seemed unnaturally loud. Lead whizzed overhead, and with a quick push Fargo was back on his feet. By then he was almost to the wagons. He hated to leave the Ovaro and his guns, but he was outnumbered and unarmed

"Stop him!" a woman screeched. It sounded like Gladiola Thimblebottom.

Fargo reached the gap and plunged on through. He turned to the west in time to see what appeared to be sparks shoot along the ground. It was a trail of black powder, poured by whoever had placed the kegs, in lieu of a fuse. Once ignited, the powder burned swiftly.

Fargo opened his mouth to shout a warning to the men from Silver Creek but it was too late.

The explosion was tremendous. It shook the trees and bent limbs. A sheet of flame seemed to rise to the stars. On its heels came the screams and shrieks of those who were caught in the blast.

Something crashed down through a tree next to Fargo and plopped to earth. It was an arm. Smoke rose from the tatters of a shirt, and the fingers and thumb twitched.

A rifle spanged and a slug struck the same tree. Someone from Lodestone had caught sight of him.

Fargo's best bet now was to ally himself with the men from Silver Creek. Once he explained, they might lend him a rifle or a pistol.

The undergrowth parted and out stumbled a man clutching his abdomen. He saw Fargo and reached out as if for help—and his intestines oozed from a hole the size of a melon. "Please," he whimpered. "I don't want to die." He took a faltering step, and collapsed.

Against his better judgment, Fargo knelt and cradled the man's head. There was nothing he could do. Nothing the best surgeon could do. "I have you," he said.

The man's mouth worked and blood welled and he coughed. "I—," he said. "I didn't think it—" The blood spilled over his lower lip, and he shuddered and died.

Fargo hurtled on. "Pike!" he yelled, taking a gamble. "Where are you?"

A figure loomed. Not the Silver Creek mayor but a stocky man who snapped a rifle to his shoulder and bawled, "It's the scout! I've got him dead to rights."

Fargo sprang. He swatted the barrel aside as the rifle went off and punched the shooter. Howling, the man went down. Fargo pulled on the rifle, but the stocky man held on.

Somewhere another rifle banged and lead whistled close to Fargo's head.

Dropping low, he raced into the undergrowth. When he had gone a dozen yards, he stopped.

No one was after him.

Moans and cries rose from those caught in the blast.

Suddenly Fargo remembered that Quilby had mentioned two kegs of black powder. He wondered why the second hadn't gone off and got his answer when he spied several figures from Silver Creek converging to regroup.

Sparks leaped from the circle of wagons, almost too quickly for the eye to follow. One of the Silver Creek men saw the sparks and shouted a warning, and they all attempted to flee.

The second explosion was as tremendous as the first. The sheet of flame lit the woods, illuminating the horror and fear on the faces of those caught in the explosion as their bodies were blown apart.

Over at the wagons, laughter broke out.

Fargo was about to melt away but changed his mind. He wanted his guns and the Ovaro.

Out of the circle rushed the men from Lodestone. Gladiola Thimblebottom, not the mayor, snapped commands.

"Spread out. Don't leave any alive. If you find Pike's body, holler."

As near as Fargo could tell, every last man had left the circle to take part in the hunt. He rose and circled, moving quickly until he was about midway. Darting between wagons, he peered out.

Only the women were still there. Thimblebottom wasn't one of them. She was with the men. Better yet, the women were at the west side watching the hunt, except for two who were rekindling campfires.

The Ovaro had been tied to a wagon across the way.

There might never be a better chance.

Hugging the wagons, Fargo glided toward the stallion. He was almost to it when he saw a rifle stock jutting from the scabbard. It must have been his Henry. For once, luck was with him.

Or so he thought until a woman rekindling a fire happened to glance over and spot him.

"There!" she yelled, pointing. "It's the scout!"

Fargo reached the Ovaro in a few long bounds. Unwrapping the reins, he swung onto the saddle. As he was straightening, a rifle boomed.

Hunching over the saddle horn, Fargo reined to the east and used his spurs. Another shot cracked and a third as the Ovaro vaulted a tongue.

Fargo crashed in among black undergrowth, came to a stop, and looked back. The women were gesturing and talking excitedly. Only one was after him.

Hortense.

Fargo wondered what in hell she thought she was doing. She couldn't catch him on foot. And she was unarmed. But there she was, sprinting madly for the spot where he had left the circle, her dress flying around her legs. He almost rode on. But then she tripped and sprawled on her face. Wincing, she got back up and kept coming.

Fargo moved closer to the wagons so she would see him. She did, and smiled grimly. He lowered his arm and she skirted the tongue and took hold and he swung her up.

"Hold on tight."

Fargo got out of there. He headed east since they'd expect him to ride west.

Hortense wrapped her arms around his waist and pressed against his back.

"Thank you," she said in his ear.

Fargo rode as fast as the darkness permitted. He wasn't expecting pursuit but better safe than filled with lead. When he finally brought the stallion to a stop, he turned broadside so he could scour their back trail.

"I said thank you," Hortense said again.

"I heard you the first time," Fargo replied. "Now what in hell are you doing here?"

"Why are you so mad?"

"That whale you work for and your other friends tried to kill me," Fargo said. "You're damn right I'm mad. And I'll ask again. What are you doing here?"

Hortense bit her lip and looked as if she might cry. "I don't want any part of it."

"'It' being the whale or something else?"

"You can be terribly mean. You shouldn't call her that. It's not nice."

"She's sure no flea," Fargo said. "Now answer my question."

"I've never seen you like this."

"You'll see worse if you don't start talking."

"Very well," Hortense said, sounding hurt. "When I say I don't want any part of it, I mean the whole scheme to take over Silver Creek. We just killed people, for pity's sake. Well, Gladiola and the others did."

"What did you think was going to happen when Gladiola came up with her brainstorm? The folks in Silver Creek would welcome you with open arms?"

"No, of course not." Hortense gazed back the way they had come. "I just never thought it would come to spilling blood. It wasn't supposed to, you know. They wanted to avoid that."

"A lot more will be spilled before this is done."

"Why should there be?"

"You need to ask?"

"You've gotten away," Hortense said. "You're safe, and Gladiola has won. Most of those from Silver Creek who would stand up to her are dead. All she and Quilby have to do now is ride in and take over."

"It won't be that simple."

"Surely you're not going to try and stop them?"

"They used me. They made me a walking target. I've been hit, kicked, shot at. They took my horse and my guns. And now you want me to just ride off?"

"It's what I would do."

"I'm not you."

Hortense sighed. "I wish you would change your mind. If you don't, things will get a lot worse."

"Something we agree on."

"You *want* it to get worse?"

Fargo barely contained his anger. "Your friends don't know it yet but they've brought hell down on their heads."

15

Fargo rarely boasted. When he said he was going to bring hell down on the devious bastards from Lodestone, he meant it. For now, he reined in the direction of the road. "We'll be in the saddle a couple of hours," he informed Hortense.

"What on earth for?"

Fargo didn't answer. She would find out soon enough.

"I don't know as I like this side of you," Hortense remarked. "You're not friendly all of a sudden."

"Tell me more about Gladiola's plan to take over Silver Creek."

Hortense rested her chin on his shoulder. "She didn't confide everything to me. Mostly, she connived with Quilby and Thomas."

"What *do* you know?"

"Well, let's see. Their idea called for Quilby to run for mayor in Silver Creek's next election. Once he won, he'd give Gladiola free rein to—"

"Hold on," Fargo broke in. "What made him think he'd win? Silver Creek has a couple of hundred people."

"Yes, but a lot of them are women and children, and women don't have the right to vote. Only a small number of men even bother to."

"How small?"

"Quilby had Thomas do a study, and they found that in the last election, the one that made Pike mayor, forty-seven votes were cast and only twenty-five of them for Pike. The rest went to his opponent."

Fargo listened with interest. For someone who claimed she didn't know much, Hortense knew a lot.

"You might have noticed there are twenty-two men with our wagon train. Every last one has pledged to vote for Quilby. He's counting on getting votes from some in Silver Creek, too. He figures that will be enough for him to win. And once he's mayor, and with Arthur Thomas and maybe a couple of others on the town council, he can do as he pleases. He'll let Gladiola open a new whorehouse, and he'll open a couple of saloons, and before you knew it, Silver Creek would be Lodestone all over again."

Fargo had to admit the plan just might work. Or would have, if word hadn't reached Silver Creek. "How did Pike find out about it?"

"No one rightly knows," Hortense said. "Gladiola suspects there's what she calls a traitor in our midst. She tried her damnedest to find out who it was but couldn't."

"One last question," Fargo said. "Why me?"

"Why did they pick you to send for instead of someone else? I heard Quilby say it was because you're halfway famous. Him and Gladiola reckoned that by having you along, it would . . . What was the word he used? Oh, now I remember. It would deter Pike and them from trying to stop us. Didn't work though, did it?"

Fargo had never heard anything like it in all his born days. Then again, as the saying went, politics was a dirty business. There was a reason no one could trust a politician as far as they could throw them. Many were only interested in filling their own pokes.

"Part of me is sorry they brought you into it," Hortense said.

"Only part of you?"

"The part that you made love to liked it a lot."

Despite himself, Fargo laughed.

"I wouldn't mind doing it again if you should feel so inclined."

"I'll keep it in mind."

Fargo almost missed the road. Turning west, he brought the Ovaro to a trot. About a quarter of a mile ahead blazed several campfires.

Hortense stiffened. "Are they what I think they are?"

"Your friends from Lodestone."

"Do you know what you're doing? We'll go right by their camp. What if they spot us?"

"Are you bulletproof?"

"That's not a little bit funny. Why not just go around them?"

"We'd lose time."

"And why is that so important?"

"Quit your damn pestering."

Fargo slowed to a walk when he judged they were almost in earshot. A hubbub in the camp had piqued his interest. He'd intended to sneak on by, but when he was abreast of the circle, he drew rein.

Everyone was still up. They were talking and smiling and laughing, in good spirits after their victory. Bottles and flasks were being passed around.

Gladiola and Quilby and others were at the fire nearest the road. Quilby took a swig, raised his bottle, and whooped.

"We cut them down to size, didn't we, boys? Now it will easier than ever to set ourselves up as the new lords and masters of Silver Creek."

"I don't like that the scout got away," Gladiola said, "and took poor Hortense with him."

"What can he do? He's just one man," Quilby said.

Mouse appeared, declaring, "Don't fret over Fargo. I'll take care of him the next time we meet up."

"That's the spirit," Quilby said.

Fargo was about to ride quietly on when Arthur Thomas asked, "What do we do about our prisoner?"

Some of the men moved aside. And there, on his knees with his hands bound behind him, was Mayor Pike. His hat was gone, and his clothes were torn and blackened by burn marks. Bowed in despair, he had blood on his face and was bleeding from one ear.

"What do you say, Pike?" Quilby taunted. "What *should* we do with you?"

Pike didn't respond.

Gladiola walked over and jabbed him with her foot. "Mayor Quilby asked you a question, jackass."

Pike looked up. "Why prolong this? You know as well as I do what you intend to do with me. Get it over with."

"Why, Artemis, my good fellow," Quilby said, "whatever do you mean?"

A lot of them laughed.

"You've won, you wretch," Pike said. "Must you gloat as well?"

"I haven't won until Silver Creek is making me as much money as Lodestone used to," Quilby said. "But, yes, it gives me great pleasure to rub your nose in it."

"You're a miserable human being," Artemis Pike said.

"It's not entirely him," Gladiola said. "The original idea was mine."

"You're just as despicable."

"Am I, now?" Gladiola said, and kicked Pike in the ribs. He doubled over in pain, and she kicked him again. Crying out, Pike quaked violently. Grabbing him by his hair, Gladiola bent and shook him so hard, it was a wonder his neck didn't snap.

"Insult me again, why don't you?"

Pike spat in her face.

Fargo admired the man's grit but he couldn't say much for his brains. Gladiola went at Pike with her fists and her feet, hitting and kicking until Silver Creek's mayor was almost unconscious. Huffing and puffing from her exertion, she straightened and said, "That will teach him."

"Remind me not to make you mad at me," Arthur Thomas joked, provoking more laughter.

Hortense chose that moment to lean forward and whisper in Fargo's ear. "What are we waiting for? Let's light a shuck before they see us."

Fargo gigged the Ovaro into a slow walk. At any moment he expected a shout from the clearing, but no one spotted them. Once he was well past, he drew rein. "I want you to climb down." Twisting, he offered Hortense his hand to help her.

"You're leaving me here?"

"You're the one who doesn't want to take a slug in the back." Fargo wagged his hand. "Quit dawdling."

"I don't believe this," Hortense exclaimed, but she grabbed hold and let him lower her. Glancing nervously about, she said, "Now what?"

"Stay put until I get back."

"Alone in the dark? What if a grizzly happens by?"

"Scream." Fargo reined into the woods and headed for the clearing. When he was close enough, he dismounted and tied the Ovaro and stalked forward on foot.

Mayor Pike was still on his side on the ground. Gladiola and Quilby and the rest continued to celebrate.

Past them, tied in a string, were their horses. The animals had been agitated earlier by the gunshots and the blasts of powder but now were calm.

Fargo continued along the line of wagons until the horses were between him and the Lodestone crowd. Quilby hadn't bothered to post guards. Why should he, when the men from Silver Creek had been wiped out almost to a man?

Slipping into the circle, Fargo palmed his Arkansas toothpick. He couldn't say what was making him do this. He didn't owe Mayor Pike a thing.

The horses paid him no mind. They were used to him, all the time he'd ridden up and down the line.

Crouching, Fargo cut the first animal loose and fashioned a halter from the rope. It was barely long enough but it would do.

86

He was debating how best to spring his surprise without being shot when fate played a hand.

Gladiola Thimblebottom stopped swilling, handed her bottle to another woman, and bent over Mayor Pike. Slapping him, she said, "Don't you pass out on us. We're not through with you yet."

"Let him rest if he needs to," Arthur Thomas said.

"We'll finish with him in the morning," Quilby said. He was tipsy and slurred his words.

"I want to have fun now," Gladiola told them. Seizing Pike by his shirt, she demonstrated her remarkable brute strength by hauling him upright and shaking him as a cat might a hapless mouse. "Wake up, you cur!"

Pike groaned in torment. The blast and the beating had taken a toll. "You rotten woman," he said. "You don't have a shred of tender mercy in your soul."

"Tender what?" Gladiola said. She, too, sounded befuddled by too much liquor.

"Feelings. Compassion. Whatever you care to call it," Pike said. "Most women do, but apparently you're an exception." He paused, and once again showed that he didn't know when to keep his mouth shut. "But then, you're not like most women, are you?"

"I'd shut up if I were you," Gladiola said.

"I'll talk to you any way I like," Mayor Pike said. "You're nothing but a tart who sells herself for money."

Fargo figured Gladiola would pound Pike to a pulp. Instead, her lips curled in a sinister smirk.

"Shows how much you know," she said. "I never sell my own body. I sell the bodies of other women." She cupped his chin and put her face practically in his. "Do you think I'd let a *man* put his hands on me?"

"What man would want to?"

Gladiola didn't seem to hear him. "Men are pigs. Men are filth. Men are scum. I haven't let a man touch me since my uncle forced himself—" She stopped and drew back.

"So that's it," Pike didn't leave well enough alone. "You hate all men because of the despicable act your uncle committed? You think one bad apple taints the whole barrel."

"What do you know?"

"I know this isn't about your uncle or your hate," Pike said. "It's about greed. It's about deceit. It's about that rotten little man behind you, who is clawing to power on your fat shoulders."

"Did you just call me fat?"

"Good God, woman," Pike said. "What else would any sane person call a hog like you?"

Gladiola snorted like an enraged bull and punched Artemis Pike in the face. He would have fallen, only she was holding on to his shirt and commenced to hit him again and again and again.

"That's enough," Arthur Thomas said.

"Not nearly," Gladiola declared.

Mayor Pike slumped, blood flowing from his mouth and nose and a split eyebrow.

Not satisfied with the beating she had inflicted so far, Gladiola cocked her huge arm one more time, then recoiled in surprise when Arthur Thomas flung his around hers.

"No more, for God's sake!"

"Let go."

"You'll kill him, Gladiola."

"So?"

"Quilby, tell her to stop," the treasurer urged.

"Why should I?" Quilby said. "The fool is of no use to us. He could have made this whole thing easy by going along. But he was too proud, too stubborn. She can shoot him for all I care."

Gladiola fumbled with her handbag and pulled out a short-barreled revolver. Jabbing it at Pike, she laughed and said, "Run."

Pike didn't move.

"You heard me," Gladiola said. "Run as fast as you can. I'll count to three and shoot, and if I miss and you make it to the woods, we won't come after you."

Pike gazed at the far end of the circle and licked his lips. "You're lying. You'll put a bullet in my back before I've gone ten feet."

"What would be the fun in that?" Gladiola said. "It's better I shoot you in the leg. I don't want you to die too quick."

"What are you doing, woman?" Quilby roused himself. "No witnesses, remember? A witness can testify against us."

"You think I'm stupid?" Gladiola said.

"Then kill him and be done with it."

"Quit your fretting," Gladiola said. "I'll drop him before he reaches the trees. Trust me."

"You'd better not miss," Quilby said.

"Don't start bossing me around again. You know how I hate that. I hate it almost as much as I hate men."

"You're hideous," Mayor Pike said.

Gladiola laughed and shoved him. "Off you go. At the count of three, I'll shoot."

"No," Pike said.

"One," Gladiola said, and thumbed the hammer.

Fargo swung onto the horse he'd cut free and started toward them. Everyone was so intent on the game Gladiola was playing, no one noticed.

"Two," Gladiola said.

"God help me," Pike exclaimed. With a low sob, he broke and ran, his legs so wobbly, he nearly fell.

"Three," Gladiola said merrily.

"Shoot him, damn you," Quilby said.

Gladiola took deliberate aim. "This will be easy as pie."

16

Jabbing his heels, Fargo rode at Gladiola and those with her. Several were laughing and a man was hollering for her to go on and shoot. They didn't hear the drum of hooves until he was almost on top of them.

At the last moment, Gladiola looked up.

Fargo kicked her in the face. He kicked Quilby, too, with his other boot, and scattered the rest like a bevy of pigeons. He didn't waste an instant but reined after Mayor Pike, who was stumbling toward the woods.

Pike hadn't looked back and didn't know Gladiola was no longer pointing her revolver at him. She was on her hands and knees, spitting blood.

Bending, Fargo hooked an arm around Pike and hauled him partway onto the bay. Pike squawked and struggled but only until he saw it was Fargo.

"What the hell?" he blurted.

"You're being rescued, you jackass," Fargo growled, and reined toward a gap.

A pistol cracked, and then another. Fargo was all too aware that a lucky shot might have brought the bay down. Or him, for that matter. But he made it through and into the woods to a chorus of cries and curses.

In less than a minute Fargo was at the Ovaro. He let go of Pike, who pitched to his knees, and swung down. The toothpick made short shrift of the rope around Pike's wrists. Shoving him at the bay, Fargo said, "Get on." He quickly forked the Ovaro. "Follow me."

Pike seemed to be in shock at the turn of events.

Fargo reined for the road. From the sound of the commotion in the circle, the Lodestone gang was scrambling to saddle their horses and give chase.

Hortense was where he'd left her, pacing and wringing her hands. "You made it!" she exclaimed as he rode up.

"Climb up," Fargo commanded. The moment she settled behind him, he brought the Ovaro to a trot.

Pike stayed with him.

For a quarter of an hour they descended steep slope after steep slope. That it was a road didn't make the ride any less dangerous. There were ruts and holes a rider might have missed in the dark. A horse could easily go down with a broken leg.

Fargo breathed a little easier when he slowed to a walk. He glanced at the mayor of Silver Creek, who without being asked brought the bay next to the Ovaro.

"I don't know why in hell you risked your hide to save me," Pike said, "but I thank you from the bottom of my heart."

"The good folks of Lodestone and me have had a falling-out," Fargo said. "If you'd given me a chance to explain earlier, we wouldn't have gone through all that and the men with you would still be alive."

"How was I to know?" Pike said defensively. "You'd killed all those men who tried to kill you. Naturally, I figured you were working with Quilby and that woman."

"You sent them after me."

"Except for the last two," Pike said. "But enough about that. What's past is past. Am I to gather you've turned against those who hired you and rescued me to foil them?"

"Foil, hell," Fargo said. "I aim to bury a few of the sons of bitches." He paused. "And a bitch, too, while I'm at it."

"Oh, Skye," Hortense said.

"Who's the young lady?" Mayor Pike asked. "Why is she along?"

"I'm his woman," Hortense surprised Fargo by saying. "And you'll leave me out of this."

"Whatever you say, young lady," Pike said. "All I'm interested in is stopping Quilby and his crowd."

"And Thimblebottom," Fargo said. "Don't forget Thimblebottom."

"As if I could," Pike said. "That woman isn't"—he seemed to be searching for the right word—"normal. She's a brute in a dress, is what she is."

"She's something," Fargo said.

"So where are you bound?" Pike wanted to know.

"Where else?" Fargo retorted. "Silver Creek. And there are a few things I need to know."

"Anything," Pike said. "You saved my life at peril of your own and in doing so have earned my undying gratitude."

"Do you always talk like that?"

"Like what?"

"Never mind," Fargo said. "Let's start with your marshal. Why wasn't he with you tonight?"

"Marshal Sadler is a stickler for the law. His jurisdiction ends at the town limits. If he'd come with us, he'd have been committing an illegal act, which he'd never do."

"But he'll defend your town?"

"With his dying breath," Pike assured him.

"How many more can we count on to put up a fight?"

Pike hesitated.

"Spit it out," Fargo said.

"About that," Pike said. "Not everyone is against the idea of the Lodestone crowd making Silver Creek their new home. A few even see it as a good thing. I brought every last man with me who was willing to make a stand. And they've been wiped out. There might be two or three left who would help us, but that's all."

"Wonderful," Fargo muttered.

"What did they use, anyway? I heard one of my friends holler that he saw sparks, and then the world blew up in my face. It was a miracle I wasn't killed."

Fargo told him about the kegs of black powder.

"Those wretched curs. That sounds like something they would do. They're as devious as can be."

"They think they are," Fargo said.

"What can we do? Five or six of us against, what, twenty or more? If I couldn't stop them with all those men to back me, what can you do that I didn't?"

"I can be smart about it."

Pike stiffened. "I regard that as a slur, sir, on my intelligence."

"It is," Fargo said. "You're dumb as hell."

"Here now," Pike said indignantly. "Sneaking up on them in the dead of night was a brilliant strategy."

"With torches?"

"We had to see where we were going."

"And let them see you."

"I'm a mayor, not a military commander."

"You have an excuse for everything," Fargo said. He reminded himself that Pike was, after all, a politician. Excuses were their stock-in-trade.

"I did the best I could. I'd hoped a show of force would be sufficient. That when they saw how many of us there were, they'd change their minds and go back."

"How the hell could they tell how many of you there were in the dark?"

"There's no need to be nasty," Pike said. "I suppose I didn't think it out as well as I should have."

Fargo let it drop. They rode in silence for a while, until Hortense shifted and coughed.

"You probably don't want to hear this, but maybe you should let Gladiola and Quilby have their way."

"Why in God's name would we want to do that, young woman?" Pike asked.

"So more blood isn't shed. Haven't enough died already? How many men did you say were with you? Plus those Skye had to kill. Is one measly town worth all those lives?"

"I appreciate your sentiment," Pike said. "I truly do. But you fail to discern the more important issue."

"Dis-what?" Hortense said.

"Namely, that Quilby and his ilk will turn a law-abiding, peaceful community into a pit of vice and sin."

"Lodestone wasn't that bad, and your town won't be be any worse."

"Need I remind you of the gambling dens? Need I remind you that whores were given free sway?"

"What do you have against whores?" Hortense asked. "They work for a living, the same as everybody else."

Pike snorted in derision. "Do you listen to yourself? A tart selling her body isn't the same as an upright woman who runs a millinery."

"That's the part that gets to you, doesn't it? That upright part.

It's not just the law. In Lodestone whores were legal. It's that sin business."

"Who in their right mind embraces evil?"

"So now it's that, too?"

"I fail to comprehend your defense of wickedness." Pike paused. "What is it that you do for a living, anyhow? Now that I've had a closer look at you and that dress you're wearing, I can't help but wonder."

"I'm one of those sinful ladies you despise," Hortense said. "I'm a *whore*." She spat out the last word as if it were the worst in the English language.

"But a couple of minutes ago you told me you were Fargo's woman."

"He's screwed me a couple of times. That makes me as much his as anyone's."

"My word," Pike said.

"If you two are done arguing about petticoats," Fargo said, "let's get back to Gladiola and Quilby."

"What is there to say?" Pike said. "We can't let them get a foothold in Silver Creek or the people there are doomed."

"Oh brother," Hortense said.

"You scoff," Pike said. "But an epidemic of loose women, liquor, and cards will bring any town to ruin."

"You make us sound like a disease," Hortense said.

"You bring diseases with you. Everyone knows that. It's why I've never lain with a lady of the night. I'd be too afraid of catching something."

"That's the real you right there," Hortense said. "You're afraid of your own shadow."

"How can you say that? I led the men of Silver Creek against the minions of disorder, didn't I?"

"And you asked if I ever listen to *my*self?"

"I fail to see your point."

"You would."

Fargo drew rein. Pike followed suit, and Fargo twisted in the saddle to stare at the two of them. "Girls . . ." he began.

"There's only her," Pike said.

"Girls," Fargo said again. "I'm sure you two could bicker all night but I can only take so much stupid. Not another word from either of you until I say you can talk."

"He started it," Hortense said.

Pike puffed out his cheeks like a riled chipmunk. "You have no right to tell others when they may speak, sir. Haven't you ever heard of something called the Constitution? It grants us the right to speak whenever we want."

"Have you ever heard of something called a Colt?" Fargo patted his. "It grants me the right to crack you over the head."

Hortense laughed.

"I thought we were on the same side," Mayor Pike said. "Why threaten me when I'm no longer your enemy?"

"Because if you don't shut up, my head will explode."

Hortense did more laughing.

"It's a conspiracy, is what this is," Pike said. "But very well. If you insist on being rude, I give you my solemn promise that I won't say another word until you indicate it meets with your approval. Happy now?"

"My ears thank you," Fargo said.

17

In the gray light of predawn, Silver Creek might as well have been a ghost town like Lodestone. No one was on the streets. The only signs of life were a couple of dogs and a pig rooting near an outhouse.

Fargo had pushed to get there by daybreak. The Ovaro and the bay were lathered with sweat. Hortense was out to the world, her cheek against his back.

"Thank God," Mayor Pike said wearily as they rode down the main street. "Safe at last."

"You won't be safe so long as Gladiola and Quilby are breathing," Fargo said.

"At least we agree there," Pike said. "To be honest, I might have underestimated their propensity for violence."

"Might?"

"You jab and you jab," Pike said.

A milk wagon was coming from the other direction, a farmer in a floppy hat on the seat. He yawned and cheerily waved, then gave a mild start.

"We must present a sight," Pike said. "I need to wash up and have a change of clothes."

"First, your law dog," Fargo said.

"Has anyone ever mentioned that you can be terribly dictatorial?"

Fargo tried to recollect if he'd ever heard anyone say "dictatorial" before. "How old were you when your mother shoved that dictionary up your ass?"

"Really now. Such language in front of a lady."

"The lady is sound asleep," Fargo replied, "and I thought you said she's a tart."

"Tarts have ears too."

"I need a drink," Fargo said.

A man wearing an apron came out of a shop and began to sweep the boardwalk. He looked up on hearing their horses, and like the wagon driver, recoiled in surprise.

"Good morning, Mr. Wilbur," Mayor Pike said. "Nice day if it doesn't rain."

"My word, Mayor," Wilbur said. "What happened to you? You look terrible. Were you caught in a fire?"

"Something like that," Pike said.

Ahead was an office with MARSHAL over the door. A light glowed in the window. They were almost there when the door jerked open and out hurried a lanky man with bony features and a tin star pinned to his cowhide vest. A Remington nestled in a holster high on his hip. "You're back!" he exclaimed on seeing the mayor. "I've been up waiting but dozed off."

Pike drew rein. "Marshal Sadler," he said. "You have no idea the joy I feel at making it home."

Fargo drew rein, too. As he leaned on his saddle horn his gut rumbled, reminding him of how long it had been since he last ate.

"Wait," Marshal Sadler said. He glanced up the street. "Where are the rest of them? Harry and Julian and Lucas and all those who went with you?"

"Dead," Mayor Pike said. "All dead."

His mouth agape, Marshal Sadler came around the hitch rail. "All of them? Tell me you're joshing. *Please* tell me you're joshing."

"Would that I were," Pike said. "It was horrible beyond belief. I'd be dead myself if it wasn't for this gentleman here. Permit me to introduce Skye Fargo."

"The scout?" Marshal Sadler asked. "The one they hired?"

"He's not as we were led to believe," Pike said. "And once he discovered they were using him, he turned against them."

The lawman gave Fargo a hasty scrutiny. He was more interested in something else. "You did say *all* of them? Every last man?"

"Why must I repeat myself?" Pike said.

Marshal Sadler bowed his head in sadness, then stepped over to the bay and poked Pike in the leg. "I warned you," he said fiercely. "I told you not to go. That it was better to let them come to us. Let them come into town and cause trouble where I could deal with them. But, no. You wouldn't listen."

"I did what I thought was best."

"He's good at that," Fargo said. "Making excuses."

"Don't you start on me, too," Mayor Pike said.

"Do you realize what you've done?" Marshal Sadler said. "Nearly all of those who were willing to fight for their homes and their families are gone. You've left us next to defenseless."

"We still have you and me and a few others."

"Not enough," Marshal Sadler said. "Not nowhere near enough."

"Quilby and his pack of vermin will be here before the day is done," Mayor Pike said. "Can't you meet them at the town limits and refuse to let them enter?"

"On what grounds?"

"Murder, for a start," Pike said.

"They didn't kill anyone in my jurisdiction and there aren't any warrants out for them that I'm aware of."

"There has to be something we can do, but I'm too tired to think of it at the moment." Pike raised the halter. "I'm going home to rest. How about if we meet here at noon to discuss the situation?" He didn't wait for an answer but clucked to the bay and rode off.

"Damn that man, anyhow," Marshal Sadler said.

"I'm almost sorry I saved him," Fargo said.

Sadler turned. "How about you? I'd imagine you want to rest up, too."

"Where's the nearest boardinghouse?" Fargo asked. He hadn't seen a hotel on his way in so that was the next best bet.

"There's Matilda's a few blocks down, but it's too early for her to be up yet." The lawman looked at his office. "Tell you what. I have a room in the back. It's not much but there's a cot for the lady. You can sleep in one of the cells. I don't have any prisoners at the moment so you'd have the place to yourselves."

"Where will you be?"

"I have my rounds to make and people to talk to. I'll be gone for hours."

Fargo decided to take him up on his offer. Reining to the rail, he carefully climbed down while propping Hortense so she wouldn't fall off, then just as carefully lowered her and held her in his arms.

"What?" she mumbled, but didn't open her eyes. "What's going on?"

"Pretty gal," Marshal Sadler said, moving to the door to open it for them. "Who is she, anyhow?"

Fargo told him.

"I seem to recollect seeing her one time when I was over to Lodestone. She was with the big gal." Sadler gave Fargo a strange look. "Are you sure you can trust her?"

"Do you know something I don't?" Fargo said as he turned sideways to cross the threshold.

"No," Sadler said. "I just remembered that her and that big gal were mighty close, if you take my meaning."

The office was small, the hall beyond narrow. It brought Fargo to another small room with a cot against the wall and a lamp on a stand.

"It ain't much," Marshal Sadler said again. "But the cot is comfortable. I have a clean blanket somewhere. I'll be right back."

Fargo placed Hortense on her side. She curled up and did more mumbling and stayed in dreamland.

Fargo yawned. He was tired and sore and his stomach wouldn't stop growling.

Food would have to wait. Sleep was more important.

The lawman returned with a folded blanket. "Here you go. I don't have any pillows, though."

"This will be fine." Fargo spread the blanket over Hortense, covering her to her chin. In sleep she looked ten years younger.

"I'd be obliged if you can wake me at noon," Fargo remarked as Sadler led him to the cells.

"Will do," the lawman said. "I'll see to your horse, too."

"I'm obliged." Fargo didn't mind sleeping behind bars. He'd been in jails before. He plopped onto a cot, put his forearm across his eyes, and was out like a snuffed candle in no time. He slept so soundly that when someone shook his shoulder, it was with considerable effort that he roused and said thickly, "Damn. Noon already?"

"Afraid so," Marshal Sadler said. "A lot has happened while you've been out. The mayor should be here any minute."

Slowly sitting up, Fargo rubbed his chin. "How about if we have our talk over some eats?"

"Fine by me if Pike agrees. There's Barker's restaurant down the street," the lawman said. "I go there all the time and they serve meals to my prisoners when I have any. Their menu ain't fancy but the food is good."

"That's what counts."

No sooner did Fargo step from the cell than the front door opened and in came Mayor Pike. He had washed up and changed clothes and must have gotten some sleep because he acted downright perky. "Gentlemen! I'm punctual as always, I take it?"

"Fargo, here, would like to get a bite to eat," Marshal Sadler said. "Have any objections?"

"Even if he does," Fargo said, "I'm eating." His stomach had set to growling again.

"Why would I object?" Pike said. "My wife made me a delicious breakfast. I am, as they say, raring to go."

The harsh glare of the midday sun caused Fargo to blink and pull his hat brim lower. "Is Hortense still out?"

"Snoring to wake the dead," Sadler said.

"About her," Mayor Pike said, falling into step beside them. "Perhaps we should keep word of her presence quiet for a while."

"I haven't told anyone," Marshal Sadler said. "Not that it makes any difference I can see."

"The difference," Pike said, "is that by now word has gotten around that the men who went with me were all killed. If their wives and families and friends hear that a whore from Lodestone is among us, they might take it into their heads to lynch her."

"Hang a female?" Sadler scoffed.

"It's happened."

Fargo had heard of a few instances where women were treated to a necktie social. "Anyone touches her, they answer to me."

"You can't fight an entire town," Mayor Pike told him.

"I can sure shoot a lot of sons of bitches."

"Yes, well," Mayor Pike said. "Let's hope it doesn't come to that."

"How did everyone find out?" Marshal Sadler asked. "I was keeping that quiet, too, until we had our talk."

"I told my wife about the debacle before I lay down to rest," Mayor Pike said. "Unfortunately, I neglected to ask her to keep it a secret, and you know how women are with gossip."

"All those good men, dead," Sadler said bitterly.

"They knew what they were getting into. It isn't as if I twisted their arms to make them go with me."

"No, you didn't twist, but you sure as hell talked them into it," Marshal Sadler said bitterly.

Fargo noticed that everyone on the street was staring. People were looking out of store windows, too, and from the windows of homes. "We're right popular," he mentioned.

Pike smiled and waved but no one smiled or waved back. "Everyone is terribly worried. The cutthroats from Lodestone should reach town about sunset. With so many of our men dead, we'll virtually be at their mercy."

"Not if I can help it," Marshal Sadler vowed.

"The same here." Fargo had no vested interest in Silver Creek but he did have a personal score to settle with Gladiola Thimble-bottom and Quilby.

The restaurant was empty, save for a lone customer in a corner. The woman who ran it was setting out silverware. She gave Fargo a menu and he ordered his favorite fare: steak and potatoes and coffee. She brought an entire pot, and as he poured his first cup, Mayor Pike cleared his throat.

"Now, then, suppose we begin. I propose that we erect barri-cades at both ends of Main Street. Marshal, you round up all the men who are left and post some of them with rifles on rooftops. If Quilby and his bunch try to enter, we'll shoot them down like the dogs they are."

"That would make us no better than they are," the lawman said.

"This isn't an issue of who has the moral high ground," Mayor Pike said. "It's us versus them."

"Pike, I can't sanction a slaughter," Marshal Sadler told him. "They have a right to a trial, the same as everybody else." He paused. "Quilby might think it's safe for him to come here since he hasn't broken any laws in the town limits. But murder is murder. You swear out a charge and I'll arrest them and hold them until the federal marshal can come."

"About that," Mayor Pike said.

"You're the sole survivor," Marshal Sadler said. "Your testi-mony can put them in prison or get them hung."

Fargo swallowed the delicious hot coffee and said, "You're forgetting about me."

"That's right," Sadler said. "You're a witness, too. So is your lady friend. Between the three of you, your testimony should be enough to convict them."

Pike looked worried. "The same thing must have occurred to Quilby and that woman, too. I could well be a marked man."

Just then the front door opened and in walked two men.

About to take another swallow, Fargo studied them. They were vaguely familiar. Then it hit him. They were two of the men with the wagon train. They were from Lodestone.

Even as it dawned on him, the pair went for their six-shooters.

18

Fargo reacted without thinking. He let go of the cup and pushed his chair back even as he stabbed for his Colt.

Mayor Pike bleated, "What in the world?"

Marshal Sadler started to turn toward the front.

By then both of the men from Lodestone had cleared leather. They weren't gun hands; they weren't that quick on the draw. But neither needed to be. They were close enough that it would be hard for them to miss.

The tallest's revolver boomed, belching lead and smoke. The slug caught Pike high in the shoulder. The mayor cried out and pitched forward over the table. The second man fired at him, too.

Fargo was only half out of his chair when he fired twice from the hip, fanning his Colt with lightning speed. The tall man was jolted back. The other one shifted to shoot at him and Fargo fanned his Colt a third time.

Both killers were wounded but didn't go down.

Marshal Sadler had his Remington out and was cocking it and taking aim. He wasn't slick with a pistol, either. A lot of lawmen weren't. When it came to firearms and shootouts, they weren't any better than anyone else except in one regard, namely, their willingness to lay down their lives in the name of law and order.

The tall man fired at Sadler.

Fargo fanned, and flesh and bone erupted from the tall man's forehead.

Mayor Pike was sprawled on the table. Marshal Sadler had a hand to his side and got off a shot at the second assassin, who fired at him once more.

Fargo had one shot left in the Colt. Like most frontiersmen, he usually kept five pills in the wheel, a precaution in case a six-gun fell and accidentally went off. He snapped lead at the second man's face. Scarlet sprayed, and the man collapsed on the floor next to his companion.

In the sudden quiet, Fargo could hear his ears ring. He was the only one standing. Marshal Sadler was on the floor, conscious but quaking with his jaw clenched.

The customer over at the corner table had taken cover under it.

In the doorway to the kitchen stood the woman who owned the place, rooted in fear.

Quickly, Fargo reloaded. Quilby might have sent more than two. He inserted six cartridges this time, cocked the Colt, and moved around the table to the front window. A lot of people had stopped what they were doing to stare at the restaurant. He didn't see anyone he'd brand as suspicious.

Marshal Sadler groaned.

Fargo stepped to the assassins. He felt for pulses but there were none. Two less he'd have to contend with later. Rising, he went to Sadler. The lawman looked up and mustered a pale grin.

"Damn me for a simpleton, anyhow. I should have reckoned they'd try something like that. They don't miss a trick, that crowd."

"How bad?" Fargo asked. Leaking blood had created a crimson moon on Sadler's shirt.

The lawman coughed. "Bad enough." He looked toward the woman. "Alice, if you'd be so kind, I could use the sawbones."

"Oh," Alice said. Shaking herself, she hastened toward the door. "On my way. You hang on."

Mayor Pike had been hit twice. The first slug had cored his shoulder. The second had gone in low in the back and not come out.

Fargo eased him to the floor. "Pike, can you hear me? The doctor is on his way."

"The brazenness of it all," Marshal Sadler said. "The massacre, and now this. I'll be in no shape to stop them when they come."

"If they get here," Fargo said.

The lawman stared. "You're only one man."

"With a lot of bullets."

"You would do that for us?"

Fargo was honest with him. "For me."

Sadler looked down at the red moon on his shirt. "My first shooting affray," he said. "It happened so fast."

"They usually do."

"I never saw anyone as quick as you. Wish I was. I wouldn't be bleeding to death on this floor."

"You should stay still," Fargo suggested.

"I do, I might not get up again." Marshal Sadler looked at the bodies. "Was it Quilby or Thimblebottom who sent them? I wonder."

"Does it matter?" Fargo had been listening to a lot of shouts and commotion out in the street. Murmurs at the window came from ten to twelve people pressed close and peering in.

"How is Mayor Pike?" Sadler asked.

"Worse off than you."

"I'm sorry I won't be of any use. It will be entirely on your shoulders."

"Fine by me," Fargo said. He meant it. He worked better alone, anyway.

"Something else," Marshal Sadler said, and seemed to gather his failing strength. "You told me they used black powder on our men—is that right?"

Fargo nodded.

"Turnabout is fair play, I've always heard." The lawman shuddered. "There's a keg over to the general store. Tell the owner I said he's to let you have it and I'll pay him out of my own pocket."

"That would come in handy."

"Another thing," Sadler said, speaking faster. "In my desk in my office. The middle drawer on the right." He gasped and bit his bottom lip.

"What about it?"

"A keepsake I've had since I was a boy. My grandpa gave it to me. You might find a use for it."

"What kind of keepsake?"

Instead of answering, Marshal Sadler melted onto his side, saying, "I believe I'll pass out now." He grinned, and did.

Fargo swore. He wondered how long the woman would take, and sat at the table to wait. His cup was on the floor, broken to bits, so he took the top off the pot and drank from it.

"Can I come out?" the man under the table timidly asked.

"No," Fargo said. "Stay under there until the next full moon."

"I only want to be sure the shooting is over. More of them won't show up, will they?"

"That's not why we're here," Kent said. "We heard about the shoot-out. We heard that you were there."

"So was Alice and some other idiot," Fargo said, wondering what they were getting at.

The barber squared his shoulders. "We think you had a hand in it."

"I shot the no-accounts who shot your marshal and your mayor," Fargo said, thinking that was what they meant by " hand."

"We're not so sure we can trust you," Kent said. "It could be you were in cahoots with those two."

"In cahoots with the men I shot?"

Kent nodded. "I know what you're thinking we should be thinking. That if you shot them you can't be."

"Makes sense to me."

Kent leaned on the desk. "Don't treat us as if we're brainless. We heard tell how the Lodestone gang sent for you. And how you supposedly switched sides and helped the mayor escape."

"Supposedly?" Fargo said, holding his temper in check.

"It's too convenient," another said.

"That it is," Kent agreed. "It could be you pretended to switch sides so the mayor would bring you here and you could spy on us and learn our strengths and our weaknesses."

"You don't have any strengths," Fargo said, "and your weakness is that you're all dumb as hell."

"Insulting us won't win you any friends," a man said.

Kent nodded. "It also could be that you shot those two to keep them from letting the truth slip out."

"You want to leave now," Fargo said.

"Not until we get some answers," Hiram Kent said, and started to raise his rifle.

19

There was only so much Fargo would abide. In the blink of an eye, he was out of the chair. Knocking the barrel aside with his left hand, he drew his Colt with his right. At the click of the hammer, the men imitated trees.

"Here now," Kent said.

"Set your rifles on the desk," Fargo commanded, "and get out of here before I forget I shouldn't go around shooting people for being dumb."

With the Colt's muzzle staring them in the face, each quickly deposited his long gun and backed off with his hands in the air.

"We won't forget this," Kent vowed.

"I don't give a good damn what you do," Fargo said, and wagged the Colt at the door.

Glaring their spite, they skulked off.

"Lunkheads." Fargo twirled the Colt into his holster and sat back down. He couldn't wait to be shed of Silver Creek but some food came first.

As if she had read his mind, Hortense reappeared, saying, "Did I just hear voices?"

"Some people came by to thank me for lending a hand," Fargo said.

"That was nice of them." Hortense fluffed at her hair. "Well, shall we go find a bite to eat?"

"More than a bite."

Fargo let her take his elbow and escorted her out. He stayed watchful for the simpletons but didn't see them. The crowd in front of the restaurant had swelled.

From remarks he overheard as he went by, the doctor was still in there, operating.

"We can't eat there," Hortense stated the obvious.

Blocks farther, they discovered another eatery. The sign read FRANK'S FOOD.

Fargo liked that. Nice and simple. He held the door for Hortense. They had the place to themselves. A man with white whiskers stirred from behind a counter and came over to take their order.

"What'll it be, folks?"

"Don't people eat in this town?" Hortense asked, with a nod at the empty chairs and tables.

"There's been a shooting," Frank said. "Folks would rather gawk."

"Not me," Fargo said. "The thickest steak you have."

"Would you like it well done or rare?"

"Just so it doesn't moo."

Hortense laughed. "You wouldn't happen to have chicken, would you? I do so like the taste of chicken."

"I do, in fact," the man said. "Keep a coop out back, so the meat is always fresh. I'll go wring a neck and get to plucking."

"No. Wait," Hortense said. "You'd go kill the poor chicken right this minute?"

"You just said that's what you're hungry for."

"Yes. But I thought it would already be dead, and you'd have the meat ready to cook."

"I don't see the difference," Frank said.

Neither did Fargo.

"I can't have you kill a chicken on my account," Hortense said. "It's all I'd be thinking about while I ate it. I've changed my mind. Is there any chance I can have eggs and bacon? You don't run out and kill the pig, do you?"

"No, ma'am," Frank said. "But I will have to crack the eggs open, which might hurt the shells."

"Was that supposed to be a joke?"

"It was cook humor, ma'am."

"Do you serve whiskey?" Fargo asked.

"I'm not a saloon, but I do have some in the back and can bring you a glass if you don't tell anyone."

"Consider my lips sealed."

Frank grinned and went to go. "Oh. And, ma'am? How do you want those eggs? Poached? Scrambled? I'd have to beat them to scramble them, and you might not like that."

"Your cook humor is wearing thin," Hortense said. "And, yes, scrambled will do nicely." She waited until Frank had gone through a door to say, "I think he's sort of snooty, don't you?"

Fargo sat back and let himself relax. "You'll feel better once you have some food in you."

"I feel fine now," Hortense said testily.

"If you say so."

Hortense folded her hands on the table and made an effort to smile. "So tell me. What are your plans?"

"Nothing has changed," Fargo said.

"You still intend to try and stop Gladiola and Quilby? All by yourself? If Pike and nearly twenty men couldn't do it, how on earth do you expect to succeed?"

"By being smarter about it."

"I wish you'd reconsider. I like you. It would be a shame for you to wind up like Pike and that marshal."

"Let's drop it," Fargo said. He was tired of her carping. Nothing this side of hell would stop him from giving the Lodestone crowd a taste of their own medicine.

"If you ask me, you're the one who's a mite grumpy," Hortense said. "But very well. I won't bring it up again."

Fargo bet himself a dollar she would.

"Although, I will say that all this bloodshed could have been avoided if the folks here in Silver Creek had a little common sense. So what if Quilby and Gladiola want to run the town like they ran Lodestone? Lodestone wasn't so bad. Gladiola keeps a tight rein on her ladies, and Quilby doesn't lord it over everybody like some mayors do."

"Lodestone was a regular paradise—is that what you're selling?"

Hortense compressed her lips. "Please don't put words in my mouth. All I'm saying is that it wouldn't be the end of the world if they took over Silver Creek. Life would go on pretty much like it did before."

"Except for all the saloons and the liquor and the gambling and the doves selling their bodies."

Hortense stared at him in disbelief. "Since when do *you* mind any of that?"

"Never," Fargo admitted. "But folks should get to decide how they want to live. And Gladiola and Quilby aren't giving them any choice."

"You're beginning to sound like that damn Pike," Hortense said, and to soften her criticism, she smiled and added, "only without all his fancy talk."

"The day I'm anything like him," Fargo said, "is the day I shoot myself."

"I'll ask you one last time to reconsider," Hortense said. "Let nature take its course and don't interfere."

Fargo should have bet himself five dollars.

"You could mount up and ride off and no one would hold it against you," Hortense refused to let it drop.

"I would."

"Why? Manly pride? Sheer stubbornness? Give me one good reason why you won't let it be."

"I'm mad."

Hortense arched her delicate eyebrows. "You call that a reason? I get mad about a lot of things but I don't go out and get myself killed over it."

"I thought you weren't going to bring it up again?"

"I'm trying not to but I can't seem to help myself," Hortense said. "It's one of the reasons I ran after you last night."

"To talk me out of tangling with them?"

"It means everything to me that you don't," Hortense said. "If I have to get down on my knees and beg, I will."

Fortunately for Fargo, Frank returned with a glass of whiskey filled to the brim. He set it down and went back.

"Please don't—" Hortense started to say.

Fargo held up his hand for her to shush. Picking up the glass, he sniffed. "Monongahela, by-God," he said in appreciation, and savored a sip. It burned clear down to his gut.

"Really, you mustn't—"

Fargo held up his hand again. He swallowed and closed his eyes and reveled in the silence. If there was anything more annoying than a jabbering female—or a jabbering anybody—he had yet to come across it.

Hortense made a sound that made him think of a goat being strangled.

Fargo didn't care. He took his time and regretted when he drank the last drop. He could do with a bottle.

"Can I talk now?" Hortense asked. "I've been patient, but, honestly."

"You can talk about anything except anyone from Lodestone or anything to do with Lodestone," Fargo told her.

Hortense fidgeted in her chair. "You're difficult to deal with. Has anyone ever told you that?"

Once again Frank appeared, bearing a wooden tray laden with plates.

Fargo's mouth watered. His stomach didn't just growl; it roared. He picked up his fork and knife and bent over his plate and inhaled the tantalizing aroma.

"Why on earth are you sniffing?" Hortense asked.

"He's a smeller, lady," Frank said. "Smellers like their food more than those who don't use their nose much."

"That's ridiculous."

Frank snorted and left.

"Now, as I was saying—" Hortense tried yet again.

"Not while I'm eating," Fargo set her straight. In addition to a sizzling, two-inch-thick steak dripping with fat, there were potatoes smeared in butter and chopped green beans. A couple of slices of bread were on a side plate. Simple fare, but a feast in itself.

Fargo cut off a piece of fat and popped it into his mouth.

"You just groaned," Hortense said.

"I was thinking of you naked," Fargo lied. "Now shut the hell up." He chewed slowly, relishing the taste.

"You're weird," Hortense said, but she did fall quiet.

Fargo ate with enthusiasm. Every morsel, every bit, every crumb, and speck of butter. It would be his last meal for a while. When Frank came back out to ask if they liked the food, Fargo told him that it was the best he'd had in a coon's age, and would he bring a pot of coffee?

"You drink too much and it will keep you awake all night," Hortense remarked.

Fargo hoped so. He polished off six cups and would have drunk more but his stomach was fit to burst.

"Care for some pie?" Frank wanted to know. "I have fresh-baked apple."

Fargo patted his belly and said, "I hate you."

"I'll take that as a yes," Frank said. "How about you, little lady?"

"Why not?" Hortense said. "I might as well enjoy my last moments with my friend, here."

"You don't know how to give anything a rest, do you?" Fargo said.

The sun was well on its westward slant when they emerged. Hortense took his arm, her fingers tightening when he said, "I'll be leaving in a bit."

"I don't need to ask where to," Hortense said. "Nothing I say will change your mind, will it?"

"What do you think?" Fargo calculated that it would be three to four hours yet before the wagons got there. Plenty of time for him to pay a visit to the general store and get to where he wanted to be.

"I've enjoyed being with you," Hortense said sadly. "I'd hoped you felt the same about me."

Fargo didn't rise to the bait.

"I can see I'm wasting my breath so I won't say another thing about it."

This time Fargo bet himself five dollars. But they reached the marshal's office without another complaint from her.

Hortense excused herself, saying she needed to go into the back for something.

Fargo sat on the desk and folded his arms. Another few minutes and he'd be on his way. The odds weren't in his favor but if a man went through life refusing to buck the odds, he'd never amount to much.

Louder-than-usual voices drew him to the window. The doctor was leading a procession. Boards had been brought, and men were carrying Marshal Sadler and Mayor Pike up the street toward the sawbones's place.

"Skye?" Hortense hollered. "Can you come back here, please?"

Fargo saw a woman come running and take hold of Mayor Pike's hand and clasp it to her bosom. Pike's missus, Fargo reckoned.

"Skye? Did you hear me?"

Sighing, Fargo turned and crossed the office and went down the hall to the small room at the back.

Hortense was seated primly on the cot, her hands in her lap. "Took you long enough."

"If it's what I think it is," Fargo said, "I don't have time." He couldn't remember the last time he'd turned *that* down.

"No," Hortense said. "It's something else." She paused. "I've tried and I've tried to convince you to leave Gladiola be, but you won't listen. You're too damn stubborn. You've left me no choice but to do what I didn't want to do. Believe me when I say I like you, and it's a real shame."

"What is?" Fargo said.

Hortense raised her right arm from her lap and pointed a derringer at him. "This," she said.

20

"You called me back here to point a gun at me?" Fargo said, acting as if it were a joke when it was anything but.

"I called you back in case I have to shoot you. It's less likely the shot will be heard out on the street."

"You're loco," Fargo stalled.

"I'm desperate, is what I am," Hortense said. "I asked and I pleaded and nothing worked. So I have to resort to this. I'm afraid I'll have to ask you to unbuckle your gun belt and let it fall to the floor."

"This won't change anything," Fargo said.

"Of course it will," Hortense countered. "The wagons will reach Silver Creek safely. Once they're here, there's nothing you can do to stop Gladiola, short of killing her."

"You're doing this for her sake?"

"You don't think I'd do it for Quilby, do you? I'd do anything for Gladiola. It's why she kept me on when she had to let the rest of the girls go."

"How about if you put that away. and we forget this ever happened?" Fargo tried.

"I can't. I'm sorry. Your gun belt, if you please." Hortense cocked the derringer. "Don't think I won't use this, either."

Fargo was sick and tired of having guns pointed at him. He believed her when she said she'd shoot, though. Slowly undoing his buckle, he lowered the gun belt to the floor. "Happy now?"

"Not at all. I hate having to do this." Hortense stood. "I'd like you to walk to a cell and close yourself in."

"You're putting me behind bars?"

"It's either that or I shoot you."

"I pick the bars." Fargo backed away, careful not to make any sudden moves. All it would take was for her finger to twitch. "Go easy with that thing."

"I won't shoot you by mistake, if that's what you're worried about," Hortense said, her arm rock steady. "I've used this two or three times before. To discourage drunks, mostly."

"You had me fooled," Fargo complimented her.

"I'm not proud of this," Hortense said. "I like you, damn it, whether you believe me or not. The thing is, I like Gladiola more. She and I go back a ways. Seven years to be exact."

"Good for you."

"Your tone is uncalled for. I'm doing you a favor. You can't come to harm in jail."

"Tell that to Gladiola," Fargo said. "Once she finds out I'm locked up, she'll finish what she started."

"I'll ask her not to. I'll plead with her to let you go if you give your word you won't ever come back."

Fargo came to the end of the hall and moved to the cell he had slept in. He was about to step in it when the front door opened and the last person in the world he expected to see came through it.

Hortense was surprised, too. "Arthur?" she said. "What on earth are you doing here?"

Lodestone's treasurer stopped cold and blurted, "Hortense? I could ask the same of you."

"I'm locking him up," Hortense explained, nodding at Fargo. "Did Gladiola send you?"

"That she did," Arthur Thomas said. "Or, rather, Quilby and her. They want me to deliver an ultimatum, as Quilby calls it." He looked around. "Where's Marshal Sadler? I'm supposed to deliver it to him and him alone."

"He's been shot," Fargo said.

"What? By whom?"

"By two men Gladiola and Quilby must have sent." Hortense knit her brow. "Wait a minute. How is it you don't know?"

"Gladiola must not have seen fit to tell me," Thomas said, closing the door behind him.

"Quilby would have."

"I doubt he knew. Gladiola must have sent them on her own."

"That's not likely. She and he have worked out everything together. She wouldn't do that."

Shrugging, Arthur Thomas came over. "You know how she is."

"That's why I said she wouldn't. She can be bossy, but Quilby is her partner. She thinks he has a shrewd head on his shoulders, for a man."

Arthur brushed dust from his jacket. "Coming from the likes of

113

her, that's high praise." His hand came to rest at the end of his sleeve. "I'm sorry, Hortense. You're a sweet gal."

"Sorry for what?"

Gazing about the office, Arthur Thomas casually remarked, "Did I ever mention that I have a cousin on my mother's side of the family who became a lawman? He and I were close when we were little."

"What's his name?" Hortense asked. "Could be I've heard of him."

Fargo sensed what was coming, even if she didn't. "Don't," he said to Thomas.

"Don't what?" Hortense asked.

"You have heard of him, my dear," Arthur Thomas said. "Marshal Sadler is my cousin and my friend."

"But that must mean—" Hortense gasped.

Steel flashed as Arthur Thomas streaked his hand from his sleeve. Fargo lunged, but he couldn't quite reach far enough to stop Thomas from burying a dagger to the hilt in Hortense's bosom.

"Oh!" she said.

"I truly am sorry," Arthur Thomas said, jerking the dagger out. "My cousin is the one I warned about Quilby and your lady friend."

Hortense was swaying but stayed on her feet. "Then Gladiola was right. There was a traitor. And it's you."

"Why don't you die?" Arthur Thomas said. "I thought I stabbed you in the heart."

"I'm pretty sure you did," Hortense said, and shot him in the face. At the blast, she crumpled.

Fargo caught her before she hit the floor.

As for Thomas, he collapsed and thrashed wildly with the bloody dagger as if trying to stab her again. Then he was still.

Hortense's eyelids fluttered. "Is he . . . ?"

"Yes," Fargo said.

The derringer was still in Hortense's hand. To Fargo's amazement, she weakly raised it and tried to point it at him and to thumb back the hammer. Wresting it free, he tossed it to the floor.

"I should have shot you instead."

Fargo didn't say anything.

"You'll try to stop them, and she might be hurt." A tear trickled from Hortense's eye. "Do me a favor. Tell her I did my best but it wasn't good enough."

"You keep forgetting she tried to kill me."

Hortense looked at the ceiling. "I'm slipping. I can feel it. I'm slipping away, and there's nothing I can do." She deflated and her head flopped to one side.

"Damn." Fargo eased her down and shook his head and stood. Two more people dead on account of Thimblebottom and Quilby. He had delayed long enough. Reclaiming his gun belt, he strapped it on, loosened the Colt, and headed for the general store.

He only had to mention Sadler's name and the owner was more than willing to help. In a storeroom at the back sat the keg of black powder. The owner told him to take it and payment be damned.

"After what they did to the marshal and the mayor, I hope to heaven you blow them to kingdom come."

Fargo told the store owner about Hortense and Arthur Thomas, and the man said he would see to their bodies.

The keg was shaped like a bucket, wider at the top than at the bottom. It had a ridge at the top to reinforce the seal. It was heavy but not so cumbersome that Fargo couldn't hold it as he rode.

The sun was about three hours from setting when Fargo left Silver Creek. Another crowd had gathered, this time in front of the marshal's office.

By his reckoning, the wagon train should be an hour or so out, depending on how hard they'd pushed their teams. He remembered a certain spot that would do nicely, and when he got there, he drew rein to study on the situation.

Fargo had made up his mind that there was no way in hell the Lodestone transplants would reach Silver Creek. Not unless it was toes up.

From where he sat the Ovaro at the bottom of a switchback, the road narrowed. Only one wagon could negotiate the turns at a time and would have to slow even more near the bottom. Woodland grew thick on either side.

It would do.

Dismounting, Fargo scanned the trees. Some tall pines on the right were ideal. He scooped out a shallow hole, then opened the keg and poured a trail of powder to where he would be when he set it off. Carrying the keg back, he placed it in the hole.

Next he led the Ovaro well away from the road so there was no likelihood the stallion would take a stray slug once the shooting commenced. He remembered to take some lucifers from his saddlebags.

Now all he could do was wait.

Fargo settled with the Henry across his lap. To the west the sky turned pink and yellow, the colors deepening as time passed.

Several does came out of the woods and grazed. They didn't spot him and soon ambled off.

Not long after that, farther up, a coyote appeared. It was there, and it was gone. If Fargo had blinked, he'd have missed it.

Finally, when there was about half an hour of daylight left, the sounds Fargo was waiting to hear wafted from above, the rattle and clinks of a wagon train on the move. Presently the first wagon appeared, the driver on the edge of the seat, his foot resting lightly on the brake as he descended the first incline. After him came a second and third wagon.

Fargo practically tingled with his eagerness to set the keg off. But he needed to wait until just the right moment.

He didn't see Quilby. That was too bad. He'd hoped the mayor would be out in front and be caught in the blast. The notion of blowing Quilby to pieces held a lot of appeal.

The switchback had four turns, and the driver of the first wagon was wisely being cautious. A heavy rig could easily lurch out of control.

Unexpectedly, someone shouted. The wagons came to a stop. Quilby and three other men came riding down the line. Quilby and the first driver exchanged a few words and Quilby and the men with him came on ahead.

Fargo smiled. Fortune was playing into his hands. He raised the Henry but Quilby was too far off yet. He'd let him get closer, so close he couldn't possibly miss.

Quilby looked worried. Maybe because Arthur Thomas had disappeared. Or maybe because the two men he'd sent to kill Pike hadn't returned.

"Little do you know, you son of a bitch," Fargo said to himself. Once Quilby was dealt with, he'd tend to Gladiola Thimblebottom. He figured that with their leaders gone, the rest would scatter to the four winds.

The wagons hadn't moved. The first driver had taken out a pipe and tobacco pouch and was filling the bowl.

Quilby and the men with him were on the third slope, studying the ground as they came.

Fargo wondered what in hell they were doing. The road posed no hazard. It wasn't muddy and there were no rockslides. Then it hit him. Quilby must be worried about an ambush and was checking for sign.

"Keep coming, you weasel."

Quilby and his party reached the top of the last grade, and drew rein. Quilby rose in his stirrups, then twisted in his saddle and hollered something.

Now what? Fargo wondered. He might be able to pick Quilby off but it was better to wait and be sure.

Quilby rested his hands on his saddle horn. He wasn't in any hurry.

Fargo willed himself to be patient. Everything was going according to plan.

More riders came down. Four, five, six. Easy to recognize by his size, Mouse brought up the rear.

They joined up with Quilby and sat talking.

Fargo scowled. To be so near to ending it, and then to have to wait. He fingered the Henry and glanced at the trail of black powder and the lucifers he had set beside it. "Come on, damn you."

Quilby was doing a lot of gesturing and pointing down the mountain.

Fargo began to tap his fingers.

The mayor lifted his reins and said something and headed back up the switchback.

Mouse and those with him started down, their rifles at the ready.

No doubt about it, Fargo realized. Quilby expected to be ambushed. The riflemen were riding point.

One thing about Quilby, Fargo reflected. The shrewd little weasel never missed a trick.

Fargo shut all thoughts from his mind and concentrated on fixing a bead and preparing to shoot. The moment had come. As they would say in the South, it was root hog or die.

21

The men riding point weren't in any hurry. Mouse had assumed the lead and made a big target. He and the outriders reached the middle of the last slope and stopped. Mouse shifted and beckoned and the wagons started down.

Quilby moved to the side of the road and stayed there, watching the procession go by.

Mouse gigged his sorrel.

Fargo did some quick calculating. Mouse and the others would go past him well before the wagons reached the spot where he'd placed the keg of black powder. He hoped they didn't spot it. Everything depended on stopping those wagons.

Mouse and the rest were moving at a slow walk, scanning the forest on both sides. They didn't appear as worried about an ambush as Quilby. One even yawned.

Fargo was about fifty feet above the road, hunkered in boulders. Mouse was almost abreast of them when another rider called out.

"How much farther to Silver Creek?"

"An hour or so, Mr. Quilby told me," Mouse answered.

"Why is he so set on going in after the sun goes down?" the same man asked.

"People can't shoot what they can't see," Mouse said.

"We have wagons, for God's sake," the man said. "It's not as if we can sneak in with no one knowing."

"Mr. Quilby knows what he's doing."

"He'd better," the man said, "or we could face life behind bars."

"I wouldn't like that," Mouse said. "It'd be like being in a cage, and cages are for birds. I'm not no bird."

Several of the men swapped amused glances.

"Simon and Primwell should have been back by now," the same man said. "If anything happened to them, if Mayor Pike is still alive and able to testify against us in court, we're in trouble."

"Miss Thimblebottom won't let it come to that," Mouse said confidently. "She told me she wouldn't."

"And you believe everything she tells you?"

"She's real smart," Mouse said. "I wouldn't have reckoned she could be, as heavy as she is."

"What does her size have to do with how she thinks?" the man asked.

"Haven't you heard? Some folks have fat between their ears. My pa used to say that to me all the time. And if I've got fat between my ears when I don't have any on the rest of me, think of how much fat she must have between her ears."

Some of the men looked fit to laugh.

"Damn, Mouse," one said.

"What?"

"No one really has fat between their ears. It's an expression, is all. Like when someone says that someone else is as skinny as a broom handle."

"Are you calling my pa a liar?"

"I'm explaining that the only thing between our ears is our brain."

"Brains must have fat on them, or my pa wouldn't have said that."

"Your pa knew best," the man said to mollify him.

"Damn right he did. My pa was real smart, too. Not as smart as Miss Thimblebottom or Mr. Quilby, but he could do numbers in his head and spell real good. He went as high as the fourth grade, he told me once."

"How high did you go?"

"Pa said I didn't need schooling. That everything I needed to learn, I could learn from him."

"Ah," the man said.

They rode out of earshot.

Fargo focused on the lead wagon. He tried to recollect the driver's name. He thought it might be Hanks.

The wagon crawled like a turtle, the canopy its shell. Hanks was poised to haul on the reins or use the brake or both. He was an experienced driver. It could have been the reason Quilby had him out in front.

Fargo got a lucifer ready. He glanced over his shoulder and saw that Mouse and the outriders had stopped and were looking back, apparently waiting for the wagons. They'd see the sparks, he realized, but it couldn't be helped.

Hanks was two-thirds of the way down the last slope.

Quilby hadn't moved. He was gazing off down the mountain.

Fargo glanced over his shoulder again. Was it his imagination or was one of the outriders staring at the boulders?

The first wagon was almost to the bottom.

Fargo struck the lucifer. It burst into flame, and he touched it to the black powder. Instantly, smoke rose. The powder hissed and crackled as it burned.

Down the road, an outrider yelled.

Fargo focused on the powder. The sparks and smoke were halfway to the road.

The outriders did more yelling and Hanks straightened and started to bring his wagon to a stop.

A rifle cracked and lead whined off a boulder to Fargo's left. He ducked as a second shot clipped another boulder almost at his elbow.

The hissing and sparking reached the keg. For a few heartbeats nothing happened, and Fargo worried that it had gone out.

Then the blast shook the mountain, fire and smoke searing skyward. The force flattened the undergrowth and brought trees crashing down onto the road. Over half a dozen, in a jumble that would take hours to clear unless Quilby had more black powder of his own.

Another rifle boomed, and a sliver struck Fargo's cheek, drawing blood. Flattening, he crawled.

"There he is!" Mouse bawled. "Shoot him! Shoot him quick!"

They tried. Slugs clipped the ground as Fargo scrambled toward the pines.

"Get up there!" Mouse roared. "Get after him!"

Fargo rose and ran. Not toward the Ovaro, toward the road.

Hooves drummed. A man appeared and snapped a rifle to his shoulder, crying out, "I see him."

Fargo shot him in the head.

Hanks was hollering now, something about stopping the wagons.

Lead zinged dangerously close. Mouse and the others were charging up the road, firing as they came.

Fargo caught sight of Quilby and others galloping down the switchback to the aid of Mouse and his men. The range was too great or Fargo would have tried to bring Quilby down.

To discourage those below, Fargo whirled and let fly with four shots as swiftly as he could work the Henry's lever. No one was hit but they drew rein.

It bought Fargo the time he needed to reach the Ovaro. He shoved the Henry into the scabbard and vaulted onto the saddle. A lash of the reins and they raced up the mountain. The stallion was used to quick getaways.

Fargo grimly smiled. He had Quilby and Gladiola where he wanted them. Those wagons weren't going anywhere until the road was cleared.

He swept over the crest of a ridge and was temporarily safe from the shooters below. Veering, he rode to where the ridge blended into a timbered slope, and once in the woods, stopped.

It was a couple of minutes before his pursuers appeared, Mouse at the forefront.

They drew rein and milled about in confusion, unsure which way he'd gone. One climbed down to search for sign. He pointed at the Ovaro's tracks and said something and quickly climbed back on his horse.

Fargo drew his Colt. He would make a fight of it.

But just then shouts rose from down the mountain. It sounded like Quilby. Whatever he was yelling caused Mouse and those with him to rein around and head down.

Fargo twirled the Colt into his holster and warily moved to where the switchback was in full view. Nine of the wagons had been winding down it when the trees fell. Now they were stuck there, unable to advance or turn around.

Quilby and others were at the tangle. It wouldn't be long before axes were brought and they set to work.

The sun had dipped to the horizon. Soon the daylight would fade.

That was fine by Fargo. He had a few other tricks up his sleeve, tricks best used in the dark. For now he hunted cover.

Presently the thunk of ax heads filled the air.

Fargo dismounted and climbed a tree for a better vantage. The ax crew consisted of eight men, including Mouse. The big stableman swung his with tireless ease.

Quilby stood to one side, watching. A table was brought, and a chair and a pitcher of water, so he could sit in comfort while he waited.

Fargo was impressed at how fast the wood chips flew. The ax men weren't wasting time. Quilby wanted the road cleared as quickly as possible.

By gradual degrees, the yellow orb to the west sank until only a golden arch remained. The shadows lengthened, and the blue vault overhead faded to the gray of twilight.

Campfires blossomed atop the switchback. The Lodestone crowd would soon be cooking their suppers.

Fargo descended the tree and took some venison jerky from his saddlebags. He wasn't hungry, but he might as well. He was on his third piece when the first stars sparkled.

Night wasn't far off.

Fires were kindled near the tangle so the ax detail could continue to work. Whenever a man tired, another was ready to take his place. Except for Mouse. He had more stamina than all of them combined.

When he was up the tree, Fargo had studied on how to reach the top of the switchback undetected. Now, mounting, he started out. The closer he got, the slower he went. When he drew rein he was a stone's throw from their camp.

The wagons that hadn't been caught on the switchback when the powder went off were parked in a circle. Cook pots hung from tripods and coffee was brewing.

Gladiola Thimblebottom moved among the Lodestoneites like a general among her troops. An air of impatience hung over the camp, and something else. Worry, probably, at the delay. Tempers were short. Twice arguments broke out and each time Gladiola intervened.

Of particular interest to Fargo was the horse string. The team animals were near the tree line, most dozing. He patted his pocket and grinned. Soon, he told himself. Very soon.

Along about ten o'clock Mayor Quilby rode up. After huddling with Gladiola, he climbed into a wagon and was in there a while, then reappeared and headed back down. Apparently, the men chopping the trees were going to stay at it all night.

Fargo hoped they did. There would be that many fewer for him to deal with.

Most everyone was at a fire, relaxing. He grinned at how careless they were in leaving their horses unguarded.

On cat's feet, Fargo crept to the edge of their camp. Only when he was sure no one was looking his way did he stalk into the open. He'd barely taken a dozen steps when two men came around the end of the string, cradling rifles.

22

Fargo threw himself flat. He aimed the Colt, thinking they'd spotted him. But they didn't come in his direction. Instead, they stopped and gazed over at the people huddled around the cook pots.

Fargo stayed where he was. He was in no hurry. It would take them hours to clear the road.

The camp gradually quieted. Some of the men from the ax crew came up and others went down to relieve them.

Gladiola ate her supper, then rose and lumbered about as if restless. She wasn't in the best of moods. Several times she snapped at people.

Fargo wondered if it had anything to do with Hortense.

A lot of the folks had turned in when Quilby reappeared. He wearily dismounted and refused the coffee someone offered. He was interested only in turning in. After spreading out his blankets, he talked with Gladiola a while. For some reason, they both kept pointing at the wagon he had climbed into on his earlier visit.

Fargo waited.

It was past midnight before everyone except the horse guards and one other person had lain down.

That person was Gladiola. For another half an hour she restlessly paced. Several times she stopped and gazed worriedly in the direction of Silver Creek. Finally she, too, turned in. But she didn't sleep on the ground. She climbed into her wagon.

Fargo let more time pass before he got to work. Holstering the Colt, he drew the Arkansas toothpick.

The men guarding the horses were tired. They yawned a lot and one couldn't stop shaking his head and stretching.

They were trudging along, half-asleep on the far side of the string, when Fargo crawled to the near side. None of the horses reacted. They were as tired as the guards.

Coiling, Fargo peered under the horses at the guards' moving legs.

The pair reached the end and came around on his side. One was looking at the stars, the other at the ground.

"Can't wait until we're relieved," the stargazer said.

"Won't be long now," the other replied. "Ten minutes, I should think."

"Thank God."

Fargo spiked with alarm. That didn't give him much time. It would be better to wait for the new guards and dispose of them, but this pair was almost on top of him. He was committed.

Fargo took the stargazer first. The man opened his mouth wide to shout, and Fargo buried the toothpick in his throat. Blood spouted as he whirled. The other man started to level his rifle but he was sluggish. Fargo slashed once, twice, then moved back to keep from being splashed.

Their convulsions were brief.

The movement and the smell of blood woke the horses. Some pricked their ears, and one nickered but none of the sleepers roused.

Fargo worked swiftly. He went from animal to animal, cutting them free.

Acutely conscious that the relief guards might show at any time, Fargo finished and moved toward the woods. None of the horses went anywhere. A bay took a few steps and nipped at grass but that was it.

Fargo hadn't quite reached cover when voices alerted him that the new pair was coming from across the camp. They didn't look entirely awake.

Fargo ducked behind a pine, slid the toothpick into its ankle sheath, and his hand into a pocket. He palmed the object he had taken from Marshal Sadler's desk. The lawman had been right. It would come in handy.

The guards were talking. Neither had noticed the team animals were loose.

Horses were naturally skittish. Loud noises would spook them. So would snakes. Rattlesnakes, in particular. The mere sound of a rattler was enough to make many horses stampede.

Marshal Sadler must have been thinking of that when he told Fargo about the thing in his desk. The thing Sadler had had when he was a boy and kept as a keepsake: a rattlesnake's tail.

Fargo shook it as hard and as loudly as he could.

The two new guards heard the sound, and stopped.

"What the hell?" one blurted.

The horses heard it, too. Every last one looked toward the woods and a few nervously pranced.

It wouldn't take much to set them off.

Leaping to his feet, Fargo waved his arms and jumped up and down, shaking the tail like crazy.

The horses erupted into motion. Unlike buffalo, which usually stampeded in a body, the horses scattered every which way. The guards tried to stop a couple, but the animals avoided them. The racket the horses made, the pounding of hooves and their nickers of fear, woke a lot of the sleepers. Men and women stumbled from under their blankets, shouting back and forth, adding to the confusion.

With any luck, the horses would run for miles. Even if the ax team cleared the road, the wagons weren't going anywhere.

Fargo was about to get out of there when he spied Quilby and Gladiola. The former was nearly beside himself, railing at anyone and everyone. He ducked back down behind the pine tree.

Gladiola Thimblebottom, though, was strangely calm. Planting herself in front of Quilby, she put a hand on his shoulder and spoke in hushed tones.

Even stranger, Quilby smiled. He called the others over and had everyone sit. Then, unarmed and with no men to protect him, he walked to where the picket line had been, picked up a rope, and did the most unexpected thing of all: he laughed.

Fargo knew he should skedaddle but he was curious to know what was going on. This didn't make sense.

Quilby dropped the rope and clasped his hands behind his back and faced the woods. "Scout? Can you hear me?"

Fargo didn't answer.

"I'm sure you can," Quilby shouted. He motioned at the empty space where the horses had been. "This was your doing, wasn't it? So was blowing up those trees to block the road. Quite clever of you, if I do say so, myself. You're almost as devious as I am."

Fargo let him ramble. Normally he didn't shoot unarmed men but in this case he would make an exception. He put his hand on his Colt.

"I say 'almost,' " Quilby said, "because I always foresee every contingency. I knew we hadn't seen the last of you. That you would continue to be a burr in our side, as it were. Which was why I was so delighted when we were given a godsend."

Fargo wondered what he could be talking about.

"We caught someone skulking about the train today," Quilby said. "Apparently he thought we might have taken you captive, which was ironic, since that's what we did with him."

"No," Fargo said under his breath.

"Can you guess who I'm referring to? How about if I show you?" Quilby turned and gestured and two men climbed into the wagon he had climbed into earlier, and when they climbed back out, they had Chester Leghorny between them. His wrists were bound and he'd been gagged.

"Damn," Fargo said.

"Remember your pard, as he likes to call himself?" Quilby shouted. "He seems quite attached to you. He's not very bright, I'm afraid."

The men holding Chester brought him partway and stopped. Each pointed a rifle at him.

"You can see what this is leading up to, can't you?" Quilby said. "Or must I spell it out for you?"

"Spell it out," Fargo yelled.

Quilby smiled like a cat about to eat a canary. "Ah. There you are. Very well. I shall explain what's at stake." He paused. "I want our horses back. Every last one. Since you stampeded them, it's only right that you go to the trouble to collect them. That sounds fair, doesn't it?" He laughed.

Fargo didn't find it the least bit funny.

"As incentive, I present Mr. Leghorny," Quilby said with a grand gesture at Chester. "Either you do as I demand or I have my men shoot him to ribbons. Which will it be?"

Fargo moved from behind the pine and took a couple of steps into the circle. "You son of a bitch."

"And the same to you," Quilby happily declared. "I suggest you start immediately. And no dawdling, you hear? If I suspect you're dragging your feet, so to speak, your friend Chester suffers. If you try anything at all, we hurt him. Do I make myself clear?"

"Clear as hell," Fargo said.

"Off you go," Quilby said, and wagged his hand.

"No!"

The cry came from Gladiola. She was hurrying over as fast as her bulk could move. "I want to talk to him."

"About what?" Quilby asked.

Gladiola didn't respond. She came up to the mayor and stopped. "Hortense," she said to Fargo. "Where is she?"

"We went to Silver Creek," Fargo hedged. To tell her the truth might set her off, and there was no telling what she'd do.

"Has anyone laid a hand on her?" Gladiola wanted to know. "If she's been harmed, all of them will pay, so help me."

"No one from Silver Creek has laid a finger on her."

"Good," Gladiola declared.

"Are you done?" Quilby said to her. "Our horses are more important than your precious paramour. The more time you squander, the farther away they'll get."

"Don't you dare talk about her that way," Gladiola said, and poked him in the chest.

"Here now," Quilby said, stepping back. "I won't have you belittling me in front of the others."

"Have you asked him about Thomas?" Gladiola said.

"Eh?"

"Arthur Thomas, you idiot."

"Oh." Quilby turned. "You heard her. What about Arthur? Have

126

you seen him? He's disappeared, and I figure it must be your handiwork."

"He showed up in Silver Creek," Fargo revealed. "To warn them that you were on the way."

Quilby didn't hide his shock. "I don't believe it. Not Arthur. He wouldn't do that to us."

Gladiola Thimblebottom laughed. "What do you know? Your good friend was the traitor to our cause. If we ever set eyes on him again, I'll personally see to it that he meets his Maker."

Quilby stabbed a finger at Fargo. "Why are you still standing there? If you mistakenly believe I was bluffing about Leghorny, I'll prove you wrong by having him shot right this moment."

"Then you won't get your horses," Fargo said.

"We'll collect them ourselves," Quilby said. "It will take longer, but we won't be stopped. Silver Creek will be ours—lock, stock, and barrel."

Fargo had heard it all before. "Keep Chester alive," he said, and backed into the trees.

"One last thing," Gladiola called out.

"Oh, hell," Quilby muttered.

"I'm listening," Fargo said.

Gladiola moved a couple of steps closer. "Hortense," she said. "Why did she go with you?"

"Isn't it obvious," Quilby said. "She ran off with him."

"I will by-God hit you," Gladiola said, and faced Fargo again. "Tell me the truth. I can take it."

"She came with me to try and stop me," Fargo admitted. "For your sake."

"I knew it," Gladiola said proudly.

"Marry her, why don't you?" Quilby said. "I really must insist that we let Mr. Fargo get on about his task. As it is, we'll be lucky to have most of the horses back by daylight. Mouse assured me the trees will be removed by then and we can be on our way."

"You're forgetting something else," Gladiola said.

"I am not," Quilby said.

"Ask him about Pike and the men we sent."

"I heard you," Fargo said. "They gunned him down. The marshal, too." He didn't mention that both were still alive when he left Silver Creek.

"Then Pike can't testify against us," Quilby said, and beamed. "Good. One less problem for us to resolve. Off you go, scout."

Fargo made for the Ovaro. Once again, events hadn't gone as he'd planned. He'd gather up their horses to try to spare Chester. Once he had, he'd find a way to put a stop to their mad ambitions.

Or die trying.

<hr>

23

Some of the horses were in a meadow where they had stopped to graze. Others Fargo came on along a stream. A few he found in the woods.

After that, Fargo roved in ever wider loops. When he came on a horse, usually it nickered or stomped. Some bolted. He let them go, for now. Chasing a horse at night through heavy timber was an invite to disaster.

Each time he returned to the camp, Quilby and Gladiola were waiting. They didn't say much.

Toward morning, Fargo brought in two more animals. As he handed them over, he remarked, "I need some coffee."

"Keep at it," Quilby said. "It's your fault they scattered. You don't get to rest until every last horse is back."

"Like hell," Fargo said, and swung down.

Several men looked at Gladiola and raised their rifles, but she shook her head.

"Let him have some," she said to Quilby. "You can see he's tuckered out."

"You don't tell me what to do," Quilby said.

"Sure I do."

Fargo fished his tin cup from his saddlebags and hunkered at a fire with a coffeepot. Filling his cup, he sat back on his bootheels and slowly drank. Gladiola was right. He was bone tired and finding it hard to stay alert.

She came over with Quilby in her wake, a minnow to her whale. "Don't take this as an act of kindness on my part."

"Wouldn't think of it," Fargo said.

"I did it because you can work faster if you've rested. I'm eager to reach Silver Creek."

"Can't wait to open your whorehouse?"

"Can't wait to see Hortense," Gladiola said. "She's stuck with me through thick and thin."

Quilby snickered.

"Do that again and I'll cut your nose off," Gladiola said.

"Time and time again you overstep yourself," Quilby said. "Why I put up with it, I'll never know."

"You put up with it because of what I'll do to you if you don't."

"Do you hear her?" Quilby said to Fargo. "Do you hear how she blusters and threatens?"

"I've fought her," Fargo reminded him. "It's not bluster."

"What a kind thing to say," Gladiola said. "I'll return the favor. You're the only man who ever stood up to me and walked away."

"Hug him, why don't you?" Quilby said.

Hooves pounded, and into the circle rode Mouse. He reined over and was about to dismount when he saw Fargo. "What's *he* doing here?"

"He's been gathering up our horses," Quilby said. "The better question is, what are *you* doing here? Don't tell me it's done."

"It is," Mouse reported. "The last tree has been chopped and rolled away. The road is clear."

"At last," Quilby said. He smirked at Fargo. "All the effort you went to, and for what? You haven't stopped us. As soon as you collect the rest of the horses, we'll head for Silver Creek."

"Why wait?" Gladiola said. "We have enough for most of the wagons and we can use the animals Mouse and his men are riding to make up the difference. At first light we can be under way."

"I'd rather have a contingent on horseback," Quilby said, "in case there's a surprise waiting for us in Silver Creek."

Gladiola mulled that and said, "We *are* sitting ducks in the wagons. Fair enough. We'll do this your way just to show you I don't always get mine."

"Where's Chester?" Fargo asked. "I'd like to see him."

"No, you don't," Quilby said. "Do you think we're stupid? We bring him out, you're liable to try something. He stays in the wagon until you're done."

"It'll be light soon," Mouse mentioned.

"So?" Quilby said.

"So everybody will be up."

"And?" Quilby said irritably.

Mouse looked confused. "And what? I was just saying. You were all talking, and I wanted to talk, too."

"The Lord help us," Quilby said.

"Leave him be," Gladiola said. "Mouse isn't the sharpest knife in the drawer but he always does as I ask him."

"Thank you, ma'am," Mouse said adoringly.

"You are aware she likes Hortense?" Quilby said.

"Shucks," Mouse said. "I like Hortense too. Who doesn't? She's about the sweetest gal anywhere."

Quilby turned to Fargo. "Do you see what I have to put up with?"

"The jackass in the mirror when you shave?" Fargo said.

Gladiola threw back her head and cackled. "He sure enough has you pegged, Quilby."

"If we weren't such good friends—" Quilby said, and didn't finish.

"Friends, hell," Gladiola said. "We need each other, is all. I need you to be in power, and you need me to earn you more money than you ever could alone."

Greed lit Quilby's features. "We'll have a great deal more of it once Silver Creek is under our thumb."

"What about me?" Mouse said. "Do I get money too?"

"I promised to look after you, and I will," Gladiola said. "When I need muscle, you're the one I'll turn to."

"You must have muscles, too," Mouse said. "I saw you fight the scout. You're as strong as anything."

"Thank you," Gladiola said. "And you're as sweet as Hortense."

Mouse blushed.

"I think I'm going to be ill," Quilby said.

Fargo drained his cup and stood. He had taken all the silliness he could. Striding to the Ovaro, he shoved his tin cup into a saddlebag and forked leather.

Quilby and several men with rifles had followed him over. "Remember, no tricks," Quilby said.

Fargo raised his reins.

"By the way," Quilby said. "I was surprised you gave in so readily. What is Chester Leghorny to you, anyhow?"

"Nothing."

"Then why are you doing this?"

"We're pards," Fargo said dryly.

"I'm confused," Quilby said. "How can he be nothing and your pard at the same time?"

"It took some doing."

Quilby shook his head. "Hell, you make no more sense than Mouse does. I'll be damned if I'd put my life in jeopardy for someone like Leghorny."

"It's the name," Fargo said. "It grows on you."

"I get it now. You're playing me for a fool. Go find the last of our horses before I lose my temper."

Fargo brought back one more before sunrise. He still had several to round up, but he had no intention of doing so.

By now Quilby and the rest were accustomed to him coming and going. The guards barely paid him any mind. He counted on that as the sun was rising.

Mounting, he left the circle. But instead of heading out after another horse, he circled until he came to the wagon Chester was in.

A guard had been posted. He was leaning against the front wheel, looking as bored as a man could look, his back to the woods.

Dismounting, Fargo crept to the wagon and slid under it.

The camp wasn't astir yet. It would be as soon as the sun crowned the horizon. He must act quickly.

The guards over by the horse string weren't looking his way. Nor was anyone else.

Palming the Colt, Fargo was out from under the wagon before the man leaning against the wheel realized he was there. He slammed the Colt against the man's head twice, caught him as he buckled, and was under the wagon again with no one in the camp aware of what he'd done. He left the man lying there. Sliding out the front end, he clambered onto the seat and under the canopy.

Chester lay on his side amid furniture and other household goods. He was sound asleep.

Fargo removed the gag. Chester stirred but didn't awaken. Fargo nudged him, and Chester mumbled something. "Damn it all," Fargo said, and shook him.

"Leave me be, you bastards. Haven't you hit me enough?"

"Chester, it's me."

Leghorny's eyes flew open and he squalled, "Pard!"

Fargo clamped a hand to his mouth. "Not so loud, you yack. You'll wake the whole camp."

Chester said something too muffled to understand.

"Keep it quiet," Fargo said, removing his hand.

Chester nodded, then gushed, "Pard! I knew you'd come for me. I just knew it. I told myself you wouldn't desert me and I was right. To think you came back just for me. It chokes a fella up."

Fargo let him think what he wanted. Drawing the toothpick, he cut the rope around Chester's wrists. "We'll have to move fast."

"You bet. If you want fast, I'll be a roadrunner. You've saved my hide and I'll never forget it. From here on out, we'll be—what do they call it?—inseparable. That's the one. You and me, pard, we'll be two peas in a pod. I've never liked peas but I've seen them in a pod so I know why folks say that."

"I should have left the gag on."

"Huh?"

"Nothing. Come on." Fargo peered out. A few people were getting up but no one was near the wagon. "Stay close."

"Like glue," Chester said.

Fargo was over the side in a twinkling. He waited as Chester clumsily imitated him, then hurried to the Ovaro. Instead of climbing on, he took hold of the reins.

"What are we doin'?" Chester asked. "You must have a plan. You have a good thinker. I wish I did, but my ma used to say I was dropped on my head when I was a baby, and that's why I couldn't ever be a sawbones or a shoe salesman. But I can be tricky when I have to, which shows my thinker ain't entirely worthless."

"We need to get you a horse."

"Why not my own then? It's tied to another wagon farther down. Didn't you see it?"

Now that Chester mentioned it, Fargo had, but hadn't realized it was Chester's. "Follow me."

"My feet are yours," Chester said.

What the hell did that even mean? Fargo almost asked.

"I lost track of you in that fracas the other night," Chester whispered. "I reckoned maybe they had you prisoner so I came and was pokin' my head into wagons lookin' for you, when damn me if I didn't poke it into the one where that giant gal was sittin'."

"Gladiola?"

"That's her. She grabbed hold of me. I tried to get loose but she has a grip like a bear. She hollered and men came running and I was caught. And then do you know what happened?" Chester didn't wait for an answer. "I gave her a compliment and she hit me."

"What was the compliment?"

"I told her that she was stronger than she looked, her being so fat and all. And she went and walloped me upside the head. About knocked me out. She hits harder than a mule kicks. How she can do that when her arms jiggle so much when she moves is beyond me? Jiggle ain't muscle. Or is it?"

"Chester?"

"Yes, pard?"

"Shut up."

"Well, hell. This is a fine how-do-you-do. You rescue me, then won't let me talk? I must say, my feelin's are hurt."

Fargo stopped and glared.

"I can take a hint," Chester said.

They moved on.

Three wagons down, Chester's horse was tied to a wheel.

"Can you get him without being seen?" Fargo asked.

"Sure. I can be quieter than a mouse when I have to be, and next to invisible, to boot. Once I was in a general store and I snuck some of that hard candy out of a jar, the kind that tastes like strawberries, and the owner was right there and didn't catch me. 'Course, I was ten at the time and only came to his belt buckle, but I still had to reach pretty high to stick my hand in that jar."

"Your damn horse," Fargo said.

"What are you mad at him for? He's never done nothin' to you."

"Fetch him."

"Lordy, you can be bossy." Chester stalked between the wagons with the finesse of an ungainly rooster. He was about to move into the open but he stopped and looked back at Fargo and grinned and winked.

Fargo motioned for him to hurry.

Nodding, Chester stepped around the wagon.

And almost immediately, someone bellowed in alarm.

24

"Look yonder! It's that Chester feller! He got loose somehow!"

Fargo drew his Colt, ready to cover Chester when he came flying around the wagon. Instead, Fargo heard him say, "Hold still, consarn you, horse. What are you actin' so skittish for?"

"Stop there, you!" the same man hollered.

Fargo ran around the wagon.

Chester had the reins in one hand and his other hand on the saddle horn and was trying to slide his boot into the stirrup, but his horse was shying, and he kept missing.

All around, people were sitting up or pushing out of their blankets. Many reached for guns.

"Step back from that horse or I'll shoot!" the man who had spotted Chester cried, and he took aim with a rifle.

Fargo shot him. At the crack of the Colt, a lot of those in the act of rising threw themselves to the ground. Running to Chester, he seized the reins. "Get on, damn you."

"I'm tryin'!" Chester managed to hook his boot and pull himself up.

The moment he did, Fargo turned the horse toward the woods and smacked it on the rump. Backpedaling, he fanned a shot to discourage pursuit and reached the Ovaro without anyone shooting at him.

Chester had stopped to wait. "Which way, pard?"

Fargo rode due west. When he was convinced no one was after them, he made for the road. They came out of the forest well past the switchback.

"That was mighty slick of us," Chester crowed.

"Us?" Fargo said.

"We got clean away, didn't we?" Chester chuckled. "We work good together. Better than me and my brother ever did."

"There's another like you?"

"My brother is nothin' like me. He's older by a couple of years and he was always bossin' me around. He liked to read, of all things. My folks scrimped and saved and sent him off to school, and he became a lawyer. I told him that was a dumb thing to be, and he said there was one thing dumber."

Fargo didn't want to ask but he did. "Which is?"

"Bein' me."

Fargo reined toward Silver Creek. "That's some family you have."

"My sister is nice," Chester related. "When we were little, she and me used to sneak off and play with her dolls."

"You can stop right there," Fargo said.

"What's wrong? They were just dolls. She had a girl doll and a bear doll. Grandpa gave the bear doll to her. Although it wasn't really a doll. He whittled it. But she called it a doll anyway. So I'd take the bear doll and growl and chase her girl doll."

"When we get to town," Fargo said, "the first thing I want is a bottle."

"You sure do like liquor. If you're not careful, you could end up with a drinkin' problem."

"I have you," Fargo said.

"You're sayin' I'm better for you than whiskey?" Chester grinned. "Why, that's about the kindest thing anybody ever said to me."

Fargo sighed.

"How do you aim to stop that Lodestone outfit? Blockin' the road didn't work and scarin' their horses didn't work, so what's next?"

"I'll let you talk them to death."

Chester laughed. "You know, that's why that fat gal gagged me. She said I talk so much, I hurt her ears. Ain't that the silliest thing you ever heard?"

"Be quiet a while," Fargo said. He needed to concentrate on how to stop the wagon train.

Chester let a whole minute go by, then said, "Is that long enough? Because I've had me a brainstorm. You had the right idea blowin' up those trees but what we really need is an avalanche."

Fargo bobbed his head at the slopes of tall timber. "We'd need a lot of boulders for that."

Chester rubbed his chin. "That's right. You can't avalanche trees. So how about we set them on fire? As dry as it is, that'd be easy."

"We can't control a forest fire."

"We don't have to. Just so the smoke and the flames are close to the road so the wagons can't make it through."

"We'd burn half the mountains and kill a lot of game."

"What's a few deer and chipmunks?" Chester persisted. "It would work, I tell you. Horses don't like to breathe smoke."

"No fire."

"Then you come up with a brainstorm of your own," Chester said. "I'm about brainstormed out."

"Good."

"What's good about it? Although I might have spoke too soon." Chester snapped his fingers. "I know what we can do. We'll shoot their horses. Their wagons won't be able to go anywhere."

"No."

"I keep comin' up with ideas, and you keep shootin' 'em down. What's wrong with that one?"

"I don't kill horses if I can help it. And they'd only send for more."

"Then we shoot those, too."

"No, I said."

"You sure are a damp blanket," Chester complained. "Let me hear your idea, then."

The hell of it was, Fargo didn't have one. He was still convinced that Quilby and Gladiola were the key. Without them the whole scheme would fall apart.

"This law-abidin' business is hard," Chester said. "I don't see how folks do it. It's a lot easier to live by breakin' the law than keepin' it."

"I could send you to fetch the federal marshal."

"That might take weeks. You said as much."

Fargo went to goad the Ovaro to a trot and drew rein instead. Shifting, he cocked his head to hear better.

"What is it?" Chester asked.

"Listen."

From back up the road drifted the unmistakable drumming of hooves. A lot of riders were coming fast.

"Are they after us, do you reckon?"

Either that, Fargo reflected, or Quilby had sent some of his men to tree the town before the wagons got there. "Are you ready for a fight?" he asked.

"I'm ready for a fire," Chester replied. "Swappin' lead is liable to get us killed."

Fargo trotted to the next bend. Once around it, he swung down, yanked the Henry from the scabbard, and moved to a tree by the side of the road. Levering a cartridge into the chamber, he sank to a knee. "We'll make our stand here."

Chester looked longingly toward Silver Creek. "You know, I've only ever shot one person. Shootin' more might not come easy."

"Ride on, then."

"But you're my pard. I run out on you, I could never live with myself."

"Go warn the people of Silver Creek."

"Don't they already know the Lodestone bunch is comin'?"

"Go warn them anyway." Fargo wanted to be shed of him.

"You're sure?" Chester asked uncertainly. "I don't like the notion of runnin' out on you."

"See if you can find anyone in Silver Creek willing to help us," Fargo said, knowing full well it was doubtful he would.

"I can do that, pard," Chester said. "If there's one thing I'm good at, it's talkin' somebody's ear off."

The sounds of pursuit had grown from a low rumble to thunder.

"Light a shuck while you can," Fargo urged, "and don't look back."

Chester nodded. "If that's what you want me to do, I will. But if you're not to town by midnight, I'm comin' to look for you." Wheeling his horse, he gave a little wave and jabbed his heels.

Fargo was glad to see him go. Now he could devote himself to staying alive without having to protect Chester at the same time.

The thunder grew louder.

Raising the Henry, Fargo breathed shallow. He had a hunch who he would see when eight riders swept into sight and he was right. Mouse was out in front, lashing his reins.

Behind him was Quilby.

Well, what do you know? Fargo said to himself. He tried to center the sights on Quilby's chest but Mouse was between them and he didn't have a clear shot. Moving to the middle of the road, he took aim again. Some folks might say that was loco since now they could see him but it also brought them to a stop about a hundred yards away.

"You!" Mouse bellowed, and jerked his pistol. He must have realized he was too far away because he lowered it and shouted, "We're after you, mister."

Fargo supposed he should be pleased that the other side had its own idiot. He waited, hoping they would blunder and make it easier for him.

They did.

At a command from Quilby, they charged.

Mouse trained his revolver on Fargo. He was grinning as if he thought it was Fargo who had made the mistake.

Fargo mentally crossed his fingers that they would come halfway and be in easy rifle range, but at seventy-five yards, they unexpectedly reined up again.

"What are you up to?" Quilby yelled.

"Guess," Fargo hollered.

"If you're thinking to delay us, it won't work," Quilby said. "I've taken steps to prevent that this time."

"You're so dumb!" Mouse shouted.

Quilby snapped at him, probably telling him to hush. To Fargo he said, "It didn't have to come to this. You turned on us, not the other way around."

"You used me, you bastard."

"To try and prevent bloodshed," Quilby said. "You can't fault me for that."

Fargo's disgust knew no bounds. "You could sell snake oil to a patent medicine man."

"I figured that once Silver Creek heard you were working for me, they'd give up without a tussle. Most folks would think twice before going up against a man with your reputation."

"They tried to stop you anyway," Fargo said. If he could keep Quilby talking, it might lure him closer.

"That was Pike's doing. He was afraid that in time he'd be voted out of office. All he cares about is lording it over others."

"And you don't."

"Go to hell," Quilby said. "It's not as if the people of Lodestone had cause to complain. Why do you think so many are helping me? They had it good there, and they want to have it good again in Silver Creek."

"Thimblebottom and you make quite a pair," Fargo said.

"That cow?" Quilby said. "If it weren't for her talent for overseeing whores, she wouldn't amount to anything. I need her only so long as she's of use to me."

Mouse glanced sharply at Quilby.

"I was the true power in Lodestone," Quilby bragged. "I'll be the true power in Silver Creek, as well."

Fargo sought to stir up trouble with, "Don't tell Gladiola that. She thinks she runs things."

"She only thinks she does," Quilby said.

Mouse, still looking at him, said a few words. Quilby leaned toward him and responded. Whatever Quilby said caused Mouse to laugh out loud. "Now I savvy. You sure are smart, Mr. Quilby."

Fargo wondered what that was about.

"As I was saying," Quilby went on to Fargo, "a man in my position has to be a shrewd judge of character."

"Like you were with Arthur Thomas."

"Arthur never did me wrong until we decided to move to Silver Creek. Blood proved thicker than money."

Mouse seemed to take Quilby aback by suddenly hollering, "Mister! I've got a question for you."

"Ask it."

"What do they call somebody who is too dumb to know when they've been hoodwinked?"

"Mouse," Fargo said.

"What? No. I didn't ask my name," Mouse said. "I asked what they call somebody who is too dumb to know when they've been hoodwinked."

"Mouse," Fargo said again.

Mouse shook his head in exasperation. "No, dang it. You're even dumber than I thought."

"Hush up, you simpleton," Quilby said. "You'll give it away."

This time Fargo didn't have to wonder what they were talking about. Riders had materialized in the woods on both sides of the road.

Here, Fargo thought he had been stalling to lure Quilby closer, and the whole time Quilby had been stalling so the rest of his men could close in.

"I'm dumb, all right," Fargo said.

25

Fargo had fallen for one of the oldest ruses in the hills. Or the mountains. The riders were trying to be stealthy about it, but on horseback that was hard to do.

Whipping the Henry to his shoulder, Fargo fired at the foremost rider on his right, swiveled, and banged a shot at the lead rider on his left. Then he did the only thing he could do; he got the hell out of there.

Racing to the Ovaro, he shoved the Henry into the scabbard, swung up, and flew to the west.

Mouse bellowed and charged in pursuit.

Fargo couldn't stay on the road. He'd overtake Chester soon and bring Quilby and company down on Chester's head.

Thanks to the Ovaro, he swiftly gained a lead. As soon as he was out of rifle range, he cut into the forest to the north. It slowed him but it would slow them, too. He relied on the fact that he had a lot of experience handling a horse in thick timber and most of them probably didn't.

The riders on that side of the road were the greatest threat. Four of them were coming on hard.

Fargo increased his lead but stayed in their sight so they would keep after him. Quilby wasn't the only one who could use an old trick.

A low limb appeared in his path. Slowing, he kicked clear of the stirrups. As he was about to pass underneath, he sprang clear of the saddle. Gripping the branch, he swung up, braced his back against the trunk, and drew his Colt.

The Ovaro ran on a short way and stopped.

The quartet from Lodestone hadn't seen him leap into the tree. They were lashing their reins, determined to catch him.

The first rider spotted the Ovaro and stiffened. He shouted to the others and sought to stop while unlimbering his six-shooter.

Leaning out, Fargo fanned the Colt. His slug smashed the man in the chest and flipped him from his saddle.

The second rider dived headlong from his horse. He landed on his shoulders and rolled into a crouch. Before he could fire, Fargo sent lead into his brain.

The third man vaulted off his animal while the horse was in motion and vanished into a thicket.

The fourth man fled.

Fargo couldn't stay in the tree. He was too easy to pick off. Coiling, he jumped. He was in midair when a pistol cracked and a slug buzzed past his ear. Landing on his heels, he darted behind another tree.

Fargo didn't have time for a drawn-out gun battle. Quilby and the others might turn up soon. He ran for the Ovaro, annoyed that tucking tail was becoming a habit. He was in the saddle and on the move before the man in the undergrowth caught on. The man's pistol cracked but the shot didn't come close.

Fargo galloped for almost a mile. By then the stallion was growing winded and he stopped on a ridge to let it rest while he scoured his back trail. For all he knew, Quilby had given up.

But no. In a few minutes there they were, Mouse out in front. The riders from the road had joined forces with those who had flanked it. Now there were twelve.

Fargo climbed higher, taking his time. He deliberately stuck to open spots where they were bound to see him. He was a kernel of corn stuck on a hook and dangled in front of fish. They couldn't resist.

At the next crest, Fargo halted. They would take a while reaching him, and he would be ready. Dismounting, he tied the Ovaro where they couldn't see it—or shoot it—slipped the Henry out, and made himself comfortable on a bump of ground overlooking the last slope he'd climbed.

They were still coming.

Fargo lay on his belly. He plucked the long stems from a clump of grass and rested the Henry's barrel on what was left. Then he set the rifle down, folded his arms under his chin, and marked the slow but steady progress of those who would kill him.

Mouse and several others were out ahead of the rest. Either their horses had more stamina or they were more bloodthirsty.

Fargo wanted all of them bunched together. They made better targets. He thought of a way to slow Mouse long enough for Quilby and the others to catch up. It was plumb ridiculous but with Mouse it might work.

Their mounts were flagging. They were city animals, used to seldom being ridden and to comfortable nights in a stall.

As they neared the bottom of the slope, Mouse raised an arm and bawled for them to stop. Mouse looked back at Quilby and then at the crest and scratched his chin as if making up his mind whether he should keep going.

Fargo chose that moment to stand. He left the Henry on the ground. Smiling, he raised his hand and waved.

Mouse's mouth fell. He reached for his revolver but stopped when he realized Fargo wasn't trying to shoot him. Pointing, he told the others. Two men raised their rifles but didn't shoot.

"Nice day if it doesn't rain," Fargo recollected Mayor Pike saying.

Mouse stared at the sky and then at Fargo and scratched his chin some more. "What are you up to?"

"Waiting for Quilby," Fargo said.

"How come?"

"I'd like to talk to him."

"What about?"

"That's for his ears, not yours." Fargo smothered a grin at the exchange that took place between Mouse and those with him. As near as he could tell, one of them wanted to open fire but Mouse made him lower his rifle.

Quilby and the rest were taking their sweet time. Their animals were lathered and about played out. When Quilby spotted Fargo, he sat straight and slowed. It was plain he was suspicious. Yet he kept climbing. For all his scheming, Quilby was an amateur. An experienced outlaw wouldn't have been sucked into rifle range.

Fargo smiled at Mouse to confuse him.

It worked. Mouse continually shifted in his saddle and must have glanced back at Quilby twenty times. Eventually he cupped a hand to his mouth to shout, "Mister, you beat all. You let us get close enough to kill you. That wasn't very smart."

Fargo was tempted to say that it worked both ways but didn't.

"Why can't you leave us be? You have Miss Thimblebottom awful upset. And I like her. I like her a lot."

"You don't mind that she has you wrapped around her finger?"

"That's not it. That's not it at all," Mouse said angrily. "She's my friend. She treats me nice and doesn't poke fun like a lot of folks." He glowered. "Like you did when you called me a moose."

"You're in over your head, Mouse," Fargo said. "If you had a lick of sense, you'd be the one who would go and never come back."

"You're trying to trick me," Mouse said, "but I stick by my friends."

It was five minutes before Quilby and the others arrived. Quilby pulled a handkerchief out and mopped his sweaty brow. "This is most unexpected. Did your horse come up lame or have you decided to abandon your crusade to stop us?"

"It's gone too far for that," Fargo said. "You never should have sent for me."

"At the time it seemed like the brilliant thing to do," Quilby said. "In hindsight, I should have found someone with fewer scruples."

"What are those?" Mouse asked him.

"Notions of right and wrong," Quilby said.

"I do what Miss Thimblebottom says to do," Mouse said. "She knows what's right."

"What about me?"

"What about you?" Mouse replied.

"You're supposed to do what I say, as well as her," Quilby said. "She and I are in this together."

"I do what you say too," Mouse said. "But her say counts for more than yours does."

"Is that a fact?"

Mouse nodded. "She says I'm to do what you say only if she says I'm to do it," he revealed.

A flush of anger crept up Quilby's face. "Are those, by any chance, her exact words?"

"Exact?" Mouse said. "Let me see." His eyebrows pinched together. "She said I was to always check with her before doing anything you want. That she has the final say."

"Does she, now?"

"We're lucky she looks out for us," Mouse said. "She's awful smart. Smarter than me. Smarter than you. Smarter than anybody."

"Did she tell you that, too?" Quilby asked.

"No," Mouse said. "Hortense did. One time when I paid to be with her, she told me how much she liked Miss Thimblebottom and how Miss Thimblebottom is always three steps ahead of everybody."

"Gladiola is a regular marvel."

"She marvels me," Mouse said.

The other men were staring at Quilby as if they expected him to do something. All he did was smile coldly at Mouse and say, "You're a marvel in yourself. I thank you for the information."

Mouse grinned. "Anything else you'd like to know?"

"Does she happen to have any plans involving me that she might not have mentioned?"

"She said once that she wondered how long you'd be necessary," Mouse said. "What do you reckon she meant by that?"

"I have no idea," Quilby said, when it was as plain as the venom in his tone that he did.

"Shouldn't we take care of the blamed scout instead of talk about her?" Mouse asked.

"Yes," Quilby said. "There are several people I must take care of but he'll do for a start."

Mouse put his hand on his pistol. "All of us at once or just me alone?"

Fargo had listened with interest to their exchange. It wouldn't take much to set them at each other's throats. To that end, out of the blue he announced, "Hortense is dead."

"What?" Mouse said.

"She was killed," Fargo said. "Knifed in the throat in front of my eyes."

"Hortense?" Mouse bunched his huge fists. "She was sweet as could be. Who would do such a thing?"

"Arthur Thomas."

"What?" Quilby said.

"You're making that up," Mouse declared. "I know Mr. Thomas. He'd never hurt a female."

"Have you seen him in a while?" Fargo asked.

Mouse looked around. "No, I sure ain't. I still don't believe you. Why would he hurt Hortense?"

"Ask Quilby."

"Me?" Quilby said.

"Why him?" Mouse asked.

"Thomas was Quilby's pard," Fargo said. "They were always together, remember? Thomas wouldn't have killed Hortense unless Quilby wanted him to."

"That's preposterous," Quilby said. "First off, we only have your word that she's dead. Secondly, I'd never harm a hair on her head. What reason would I have? I like her."

"Is that true, Mouse?" Fargo fed the flame of doubt he'd kindled. "Does Quilby like Hortense as much as you do?"

"No one does," Mouse declared. He turned to Quilby. "It is strange, that Thomas fella vanishing like he did."

"I don't know where Arthur got to," Quilby said. "I'm as much in the dark as you are."

"Or Quilby could be lying," Fargo suggested.

"You're the damn liar here," Quilby barked. "Don't you think I see what you're up to? You're trying to set him against me."

"I wish Miss Thimblebottom was here," Mouse said. "She'd know what to do."

"Hortense was her friend," Fargo said. "She wouldn't let Quilby get away with having Thomas kill her."

"Damn you," Quilby said.

"No, she wouldn't," Mouse said.

"Don't listen to him," Quilby urged. "He's provoking you in the hope that you'll eliminate me and save him the trouble."

"All I want," Fargo said, "is to have Hortense rest easy in her grave."

"I want that too," Mouse said.

Quilby's temper exploded. He rounded on Mouse with, "You infernal idiot. You're being manipulated, and you're too stupid to realize it. You think Gladiola is the brains in our group? I have news for you. This whole scheme was *my* idea. She would have gone off to Denver with the rest of her doves if I hadn't mentioned I had a plan for taking over Silver Creek. *I'm* the brains, not her. From now on you're to do what I say and not what she says. Do you hear me, you simpleton? Have I gotten through that thick skull of yours?"

"You shouldn't ought to talk to me like that."

"I'll talk to you any damn way I please," Quilby raged. "I've had enough of you and, by-God, I've had enough of her, too. When we get back I'm giving Gladiola a piece of my mind. She's gone too far."

"So have you," Mouse said, and pulled his pistol.

26

Two men from Lodestone jerked their own smoke wagons and leveled them at Mouse.

"What in hell do you think you're doing?" one said.

"Quit pointing that six-shooter at Quilby," the other warned, "or we'll shoot you where you sit."

"Stay out of this," Mouse said.

"The mayor is right," the first man said. "The scout is trying to turn you against us."

"Use your damn head, you infant," the other said.

"I've done used it already. It told me I'm being lied to," Mouse said. "And I'm not no infant. I'm too big for diapers."

"You can say that again," Quilby said. "But it's good to hear you've come to your senses." He paused. "Why are you still pointing that revolver at me? You just said that you know you're being lied to."

"I do," Mouse said, nodding slowly, "and you're the polecat who's lying." With that he shot Quilby in the forehead.

The others froze in disbelief. The first to regain their wits were the pair pointing six-guns at Mouse. One fired just as Mouse swung his sorrel around. Mouse clubbed him, whipped the other way, and clubbed the second man. Both dropped like rocks.

The rest weren't sure what to do. They stared at Quilby's body and at Mouse and back again.

"What have you done?" one said.

"He had Hortense killed," Mouse answered.

"You stupid bastard."

Mouse lost all control. He jabbed his heels into his mount and flew in among them, striking right and left. A bull among calves, he felled fully half. One man punched him but the blow had no effect. Another man clawed at a six-gun but Mouse stove in his forehead.

The few who were still able to fled.

By then Fargo had scooped up the Henry and was running down the slope. No one paid any attention to him.

Mouse glared after the men riding off. "Go on back to the wagon train, you weak sisters. And you'd better listen to Miss Thimblebottom—you hear me?" He shook his revolver at them. "If you don't, you'll answer to me."

Fargo slowed and held the Henry close to his leg. Thumb-cocking the hammer, he said, "Who do I answer to?"

Mouse looked over his shoulder with no more concern than if Fargo was holding a stick. "Miss Thimblebottom, the same as every-body. And she wants you dead."

Fargo tensed to sweep the Henry up and shoot but in a twinkling Mouse spun and dived from his horse. Fargo sidestepped, or tried to. The six-gun clipped him, knocking his hat off and causing him to stagger. Before he could recover his balance, Mouse was on him.

It was their fight in Lodestone all over again, only this time Mouse used his head as well as his fists.

Fargo was slow in getting his arms up to block and was jolted to his marrow by a blow to the ribs. He landed a punch of his own but Mouse acted as if he didn't feel it. Fargo set himself as Mouse let fly with a flurry that would have battered most men to their knees. Fargo absorbed the punishment on his forearms. When Mouse drove a fist at his jaw, he ducked and retaliated with an uppercut. It lifted Mouse onto his bootheels. Seizing the advantage, Fargo landed two more uppercuts. They about broke his hand but they also knocked Mouse onto his back.

For a few moments Fargo had the illusion he had knocked Mouse out.

Roaring like an enraged grizzly, Mouse heaved to his feet. Fargo met him with a cross to the cheek. The cheek split but Mouse kept coming.

Spreading his arms, Mouse clutched Fargo in a bear hug, pinning Fargo's arms to his side.

"Got you now," Mouse gloated. "Gonna break your bones." He gritted his teeth and his jaw muscles flexed.

To Fargo, it felt as if he were being crushed. His chest exploded with pain and his senses swam. Quickly, he smashed his fore-head into Mouse's face. He did it once, twice. Mouse's nose crunched and blood sprayed but Mouse continued to apply that awful, deadly pressure.

Fargo slammed his forehead into Mouse's mouth. Mouse

howled and redoubled his effort. Fargo slammed and slammed again. Wet drops splattered his face. He drew back his head one more time and gave it all he had. It about cracked his skull but it also caused Mouse to let go and totter.

Fargo fell to his knees. Instinctively, he groped at his pant leg and his boot. The Arkansas toothpick was his last resort. Before he could slide the blade free, Mouse's thick fingers wrapped around his neck, gouging deep as Mouse applied incredible pressure.

"Gonna choke you to death, you son of a bitch."

With his free hand Fargo pried at Mouse's fingers but he was too weakened to loosen them.

Mouse had a bloody grin on his face. "Miss Thimblebottom will be pleased with me."

Fargo felt Mouse's fingers gouge deeper. His breath had been cut off and his lungs screamed for air. He managed to slide the toothpick out, and in a desperate lunge, he drove it into Mouse's throat and slashed from side to side.

Mouse was slow to realize it. He looked down at the scarlet-smeared knife in Fargo's hand and started to say something and blood gushed from his mouth. Panic overcame him. Pushing away, he clasped both hands to his neck but there was no staunching the crimson river. He gulped like a fish out of water and reached for empty air.

No, Fargo realized. Not for air. Mouse was reaching in the direction of the wagon train and Gladiola Thimblebottom. He watched without sympathy as Mouse folded in on himself, sprawled forward, and broke into convulsions. The spark of life fled his wide eyes and he was still.

Fargo sucked in a deep breath. It had been a close thing. He wiped the toothpick on the grass and stared in the same direction Mouse had been reaching.

"I'm coming for you, bitch."

27

No clearings were handy so the wagons had stopped in the middle of the road. Over half were missing their teams. Evidently some of the Lodestone crowd had had enough of bullets and bloodshed and fled on horseback.

Some, but not all.

Fargo was well out of rifle range when a rifle cracked. The lead fell short. It served as a warning. Not that he needed one. Gladiola wouldn't give up without a fight.

She wasn't the type.

Entering the woods, Fargo rode in a wide loop. How many he was up against was anyone's guess. He didn't think it could be more than seven or eight, which was still more than enough to make worm food of him if he wasn't careful. He shucked the Henry and jacked the lever.

The wagons appeared deserted. A hint of movement under one and the glint of metal in another proved otherwise.

Drawing rein, Fargo dismounted. No shots were fired. They might have lost track of him amid the trees. Acting on that assumption, he glided forward until he was close enough to see the man under the wagon.

Whoever he was, he had a Spencer, and he was nervous. He twisted and turned and couldn't lie still.

Fargo braced the Henry against an oak. He had a hunch that first shot had been courtesy of the nervous gent, and he figured to repay the favor. A wagon wheel made aiming for the head or chest an iffy proposition so he fixed the Henry's sights on the man's hip. The moment the man paused in his fidgeting, Fargo fired.

A howl greeted the blast. The man flipped onto his back, then scrambled to get out from under the wagon on the other side. He was on one knee when Fargo put lead into it.

Others awoke to the plight of their companion. An uneven volley from rifles and revolvers drove Fargo to ground as slugs clipped leaves and sent slivers of bark flying.

When it was safe to raise his head again, the man under the wagon had disappeared.

Another shooter was in the next wagon up the line. Fargo had seen him pop out and fire. Fargo trained the Henry on the canopy and banged off a couple of shots. A yelp showed how close he came. But the man didn't pop out again.

Fargo could keep this up all day. The Lodestone crowd wasn't going anywhere with so many of their horses missing. They had set a trap for him but now they were the ones who were trapped. They were stuck there unless they had mounts hidden nearby.

Moving to his left, Fargo sought another target. He hadn't gone far when he heard the crackle of underbrush. Someone was stalking *him*. And not from the vicinity of the wagons, either. They were coming up behind him.

Wondering if Gladiola had told some of her men to fan out in the woods before he got there, Fargo twisted around. Whoever it was, they were awful at it. An Apache would have laughed them to scorn. A head appeared and looked around, seeking him. He stayed where he was until the man was practically on top of him, then said quietly, "What in hell are you doing here?"

Chester Leghorny nearly jumped out of his boots. "Pard!" he exclaimed. "Don't do that."

"I sent you to Silver Creek," Fargo said. So he could be safe from harm, he could have added but didn't.

"I headed there," Chester said. "You saw me leave, remember?"

"You lost your way?"

Chester blinked. "What? No. I got to thinkin' how you were fixin' to tangle with this bunch by yourself and how it was wrong of me to run out on you when you needed me most so I turned around and here I am."

"I wish you hadn't," Fargo said.

"I saw you come out of the woods a ways back and ride up the road and then go into the woods again, and I snuck in after you. How'd you know I was sneakin' up on you, anyhow?"

"I thought it was a buffalo."

"Why would a buff be sneakin' around these woods?" Chester shook his head. "Sometimes, pard, you make no sense." He gazed toward the wagons. "So how do we do this? Rush 'em and wipe 'em out?"

"I was thinking I'd pick them off one at a time."

"Oh. You want to do it the hard way. That's fine by me." Chester grinned. "Let's start the pickin'."

"I don't suppose I can talk you into watchin' our horses until it's over?"

"What kind of pard would I be to let you do all the fightin'? No, we are in this together. From now on I won't ever leave your side."

"Wonderful."

"You don't sound too happy about it."

"Chester, listen. . . ." Fargo was going to explain that he could fight better not having to look out for him, too, when midway between them and the Conestogas some brush swayed. Putting a finger to his lips, he motioned for Chester to flatten.

Looking puzzled, Chester did.

The brush stopped moving. Soon a patch of gambel oak rustled but it was thirty feet away and couldn't be the same man.

Fargo held up two fingers to let Chester know there were two of them.

Chester held up two fingers of his own and looked at them and then at Fargo and smiled. "The two of us, together," he happily whispered.

"No. There are two men stalking us."

"There are?" Chester peered into the vegetation. "I don't see them."

"Trust me. They're there. Now hush and get ready."

"I was born ready, pard," Chester said. "Look out, Thimbletits. Here we come." He actually giggled. "This is goin' to be fun."

28

A rifle blasted and the slug clipped Chester's hat, almost knocking it off. Chester bleated and pressed his cheek to the ground, saying, "That was close!"

A puff of smoke in the oaks gave the shooter's position away. Fargo fired twice.

The other man opened up, and for over a minute they swapped

lead. In a lull, Fargo quickly began reloading the Henry's tubular magazine.

"Did you get them?" Chester whispered.

"Not yet," Fargo said.

"What are you waitin' for?"

Fargo went on reloading.

"I have an idea," Chester said.

"No."

"You ain't heard it yet."

"The answer is still no."

"I'll crawl off a bit and shoot at them to draw their fire and you can pick them off before they pick me off."

Fargo stared.

"I reckoned you really wanted to hear it."

Not far off, the vegetation moved. The pair were closing in.

The man in the oaks was closer, and Fargo concentrated on him. A silhouette appeared but was gone before he could shoot.

"I have another trick," Chester whispered. "I can chuck rocks and they'll shoot at where I chuck 'em and you can pick 'em off that way."

Fargo bent toward him and without taking his eyes off the oaks, he said, "Shut . . . the . . . hell . . . up."

A rifle barrel gleamed in a shaft of sunlight. Fargo rolled as the rifle boomed, rose on his elbows, and banged a shot in return. The barrel had already vanished. Whoever these two were, they were good. He crawled to a log, removed his hat, and peered over.

The woods and the wagons beyond were deceptively quiet.

Fargo moved to the end of the log and carefully looked around it. Still nothing. He decided to lie there and let them come to him. Waving stems of grass gave him warning that one was on the move. He slowly extended the Henry. When the stems parted and a man's bearded face poked out, he stroked the trigger. A scarlet splotch blossomed between the man's eyes.

The other one cut loose, raking the log. Fargo was forced to hug the earth. He heard Chester's rifle boom and the man answered. Rolling away from the log and into some skunkbush, Fargo raised his head for a quick look-see. The second rifleman was behind a hawthorn. In the blink of an eye Fargo aimed and fired. The impact doubled the rifleman over. Fargo's next shot brought him crashing down.

New silence fell.

Reclaiming his hat, Fargo snaked to where he'd left his so-called pard. Chester was gone. Flattened grass pointed toward the road.

The simpleton had no more brains than a chipmunk. Fargo fumed, and went after him.

Sunlight and shadows dappled the wagons. The men who were left—and Gladiola—weren't taking any chances. They were lying low.

Fargo glimpsed Chester, crabbing much too quickly. It was a wonder he wasn't shot.

The canopy on a Conestoga bulged slightly, and a long, dark object slid out. A rifle barrel, Fargo realized, pushed through a cut in the canvas. He aimed at where he judged the man must be and sent three rounds crashing through it. The rifle barrel swung crazily, then tilted at the sky and stayed there.

Chester raised his head and looked back. Fargo gestured for him to stay where he was but Chester grinned and kept on crawling.

Fargo hurried to overtake him.

A shape filled the back of a wagon. An arm and a pistol were pointed at Chester, who was looking the other way.

Snapping a shot, Fargo worked the Henry's lever and fired a second time. The shape fell back. Then a hand gripped the top of the end gate and a head and shoulders slumped over it.

Chester saw, and fired. He missed. He went to shoot again but the man was sliding over the gate, already dead.

Fargo took a gamble. Heaving up, he raced to Chester, grabbed him by the scruff of his collar, and pulled him to his feet.

"What the hell?" Chester squawked.

A rifle cracked. And another. Propelling Chester toward the nearest wagon, Fargo couldn't return fire. He made it there and shoved Chester under and was diving under it himself when a slug struck the side with a loud thwack.

"Were you tryin' to get us shot?" Chester complained.

Ignoring him, Fargo searched for the shooters. One was up the line, the other down it somewhere.

"That was a damned silly stunt, pard." Chester wouldn't let it drop. "What were you thinkin'?"

"The next time I'll let them kill you." Fargo thought he saw a foot near a wagon wheel but it vanished.

"None of them knew where I was until you grabbed me," Chester said. "If there's one thing I'm good at, it's bein' sneaky."

"You're even better at being stupid."

"Honestly, pard. You pick the strangest times to crack jokes."

Fargo tried to put himself in the boots of those out to kill him. Would they be content to bide their time and let him make the next move? Or would they try to get in close to finish it. Furtive movement gave him his answer. "They're coming for us," he whispered.

"I sure as blazes hope so," Chester said. "I want this over with so you and me can light a shuck for Denver and have us a high old time."

Fargo set the Henry down and drew his Colt.

"I've got it all planned," Chester said. "We'll have a shave and a bath and do the town right. You might want to get rid of that beard. I had a gal tell me once that ladies like smooth chins, not hairy ones. She was kind of hairy herself, so that might be why. But still. . ."

A man in a striped shirt was coming around a wagon. Unlike the others, he was armed with a shotgun.

"And don't forget to polish your boots," Chester said. "Nothin' impresses a female more than shiny stuff. Jewelry, boots, chins, you name it."

Fargo couldn't afford to miss. One blast from that hand howitzer, and both he and gabby mouth would be blown to pieces. He aimed between two spokes at the man's head.

"Money impresses them too," Chester was saying while looking out the other side. "Which always struck me as a feeble reason to like someone. What's a fella with money got that a fella without money doesn't? Why not just like a man for who he is?"

Fargo was going to tell him to shut up but what would have been the use?

"Between you and me, I never have understood females. I reckon it's that 'fe' business. If they were just males I'd savvy them better."

The man with the shotgun spotted Chester and eased up to shoot.

29

Fargo fired first.

The shotgun went off and the wagon above them seemed to shake to the impact.

Chester yelped and flung himself down, shouting, "Someone's shootin' at us!"

Fargo didn't know what to make of what happened next. A Lodestoneite rushed from behind a tree, firing as he came. Maybe it was desperation. Maybe the man thought he could hit them before they got him. Fargo proved him wrong.

"Good shootin'," Chester said. "I would have done it if I'd seen him."

Fargo hurriedly replaced the spent cartridges. He spun the cylinder and looked right but saw no one and looked left and saw no one and looked past the wagon wheel and was jarred by surprise. He pointed the Colt but didn't shoot.

Gladiola Thimblebottom had appeared out of thin air, her empty hands raised. "I give up," she hollered. "Don't shoot."

Chester trained his rifle and said, "Look at her! As big as anything. What's she up to?" He started to slide out but Fargo grabbed his arm.

"There might be others."

Gladiola heard him. "I'm all that's left," she informed them. "I know when I'm licked and I'm surrendering."

"By golly, we did it," Chester said, and made as if to slide out from under the wagon.

"Wait." Fargo suspected she was up to something. She wouldn't give up this easily. Not her.

Gladiola slowly came toward them, her dress flapping in a gust of wind. "I'm telling the truth," she said. "I wouldn't be doing this if I weren't."

"Stop where you are," Fargo snapped, and she did.

"At least she listens good," Chester said.

They waited but heard only the rustle of canvas and the nicker of a team horse farther up.

"Where are they if there are any?" Chester wondered.

"I told you it's just me," Gladiola said. "Everyone else lit out. Take me to Silver Creek and this will be over."

"I like that idea," Chester said. Before Fargo could stop him, he was out and standing and gazing all about. "She must be tellin' the truth, pard. I don't see anybody anywhere."

Against his better judgment, Fargo grabbed the Henry and rose from under the bed. No shots thundered. Still not convinced, he warily moved around behind Gladiola and pressed the Colt's muzzle to her broad back. "Find some rope," he said to Chester.

"Will do, pard."

"You're pards, are you?" Gladiola said as Leghorny eagerly ran up the line.

"He thinks we are."

"Speaking of which," Gladiola said. "Where's my Hortense?"

"You haven't heard?" Fargo stalled, debating whether to tell her.

"Would I have asked if I had?" Gladiola looked over her shoulder at him. "Where is she, damn you? Nothing better have happened to her or there will be hell to pay."

Fargo decided she might as well know. Since it wasn't his doing, she had no cause to take it out on him. "Arthur Thomas killed her. He was the spy in your outfit. The Silver Creek marshal was his cousin."

"Hortense is dead?"

"Thomas stabbed her."

"Hortense is dead," Gladiola said, all the life gone out of her voice.

"She was about to put me behind bars and keep me there until you showed up," Fargo said. He looked after Chester, who had hopped onto a wagon and stuck his head under the canvas.

"She and I were together a long time. I'd have done anything for her and she'd have done anything for me."

Fargo grunted, wishing the simpleton would hurry.

"Now that she's gone," Gladiola said, "the least I can do is avenge her."

Fargo didn't like the sound of that. "Avenge her how? Arthur Thomas is dead. She shot him."

"Good for her," Gladiola said proudly. She coughed, then said, "Not avenge her directly. But take revenge on the cause of all this. On the fly in our ointment."

"I've got a gun to your back," Fargo reminded her. Chester had hopped down and was moving to the next wagon.

"There comes a time when you just don't care," Gladiola said. "When you do what you have to and the consequences be damned. Haven't you ever felt that way about something or other?"

"Yes," Fargo admitted.

"Quilby and I had this all planned out. It would have worked except for you. You weren't what we expected. You have a conscience."

"It's there somewhere," Fargo said.

"We didn't figure you to have one. Not with all the talk about your womanizing and drinking and fondness for cards. We figured you'd be happy to help us."

"You figured wrong."

"What was it exactly that turned you against us? I'd really like to know."

156

"You made me a target," Fargo told her. "I had assassins coming out of nowhere."

"And you took that personal?" Gladiola nodded. "I suppose I can't blame you. I take Hortense personal, too. Which is why I'm going to strangle you with my bare hands."

Fargo had glanced toward Chester again. He started to turn but Gladiola, for all her bulk, was incredibly quick. She spun and gripped his wrist even as her other hand clamped onto his throat.

"I will kill you dead," she hissed.

Fargo had almost forgotten how immensely strong she was. Her hand on his wrist squeezed harder and she pushed his arm to one side so if the Colt went off, she wouldn't take the slug. In the same motion, she dug her fingers into his neck with renewed force.

"Dead, dead, dead."

Struggling, Fargo took a step back. Gladiola clung fast. She was fury incarnate, her eyes glittering points of pure hate, her mouth a slit. She suddenly rammed into him, knocking him off his feet, and in another moment he was on his back on the ground and she came down on him like a ten-ton boulder, her thick knees slamming onto his hips. It was like having a Conestoga fall on top of him.

Fargo tore at the hand on his throat. He punched her on the jaw.

"You won't stop me this time."

Fargo drove his fist at her throat but she had tucked her chin to protect it. He struck her cheek, her temple. He might as well be battering a tree. She grinned and bore down with all her weight and strength.

Fargo bucked, or tried to. She was so heavy, he couldn't rise up off the ground. He couldn't knee her in the back, either. She was straddling his hips but her ample backside was on his legs, pinning them. His chest began to hurt. He hadn't had time to suck in a breath when she grabbed him. His neck felt as if it was about to be rendered to pulp.

She was killing him.

Fargo gouged a finger at her eye but she jerked her face away. He tried again and she bit at his finger.

There had to be something he could do. He boxed her ear. He clubbed her head. He punched her chest, her side. She absorbed the punishment like a sponge. And then she did something frightening. She smiled.

Fargo's life was on the cusp of fading. His ears roared with the blood in his veins, and when he heard thunder, he thought it must have been his imagination. Simultaneously, part of Gladiola's head exploded, showering skin and bone and gore. Her eyes rolled up into their sockets, her grip slackened, and she collapsed on top of him.

Gasping for air, Fargo had to try three times to shove her off. He sat up, propped himself on his hands, and sucked in deep breaths.

Chester stood a few yards away, his smoking six-gun in his hand. He looked at it and at Thimblebottom. "I shot her."

Fargo had to force his throat to work. "I'm . . ." he rasped out, ". . . obliged."

"I should feel good that I shot her but I don't." Frowning, Chester slid the six-shooter into his holster. "I don't think I'll shoot anybody anymore. It's not as much fun as I thought it would be." He stared at the body, then brightened. "Say. I just realized. Is it over? Can we go to Denver now, pard?"

"Denver . . ." Fargo said, ". . . sounds fine."

LOOKING FORWARD!
The following is the opening
section of the next novel in the exciting
Trailsman series from Signet:

TRAILSMAN #393
SIX-GUN INFERNO

1861—the sunbaked desert of southwestern Nevada,
where a bullet to the brain is the least of a man's worries.

The rider was a red-hot coal, his lungs a furnace. When he breathed, he swore he inhaled fire. The desert country of Nevada Territory was no place to be in the hottest month of the summer.

Skye Fargo drew rein and squinted from under his hat's brim at the blazing source of his discomfort. "Where's a cloud when you need one?" he grumbled at the clear blue sky.

Fargo reached for his canteen but thought better of it. There was barely a third left, and he had a lot of miles to cover.

A big man, broad at the shoulders, he wore buckskins and a white hat so coated with dust, it looked to be brown. A well-worn Colt hung at his waist, a red bandanna added color to his neck. He swallowed, or tried to, and grimaced at how dry his throat had become. "The next time I say I want to take a shortcut," he said to his horse, "kick me."

The Ovaro twitched an ear. Head hung low, lathered with sweat, the stallion needed water more than Fargo. He patted its neck and said, "We'll get you a drink soon, big fella."

Or so Fargo hoped. The truth was, he'd decided to cut across a section of desert he'd never been through before, and now here he was, miles from anywhere, in the middle of an expanse of sand dunes and flats where the earth had been baked dry of life.

Fargo gigged the Ovaro into motion. He tried not to dwell on the last three creek beds they'd come across. The creeks only ran with water in the winter. Now they were as dry as his mouth.

The stallion plodded on.

Fargo bowed his head and closed his eyes. He imagined being in a saloon in the cool of evening with a saucy dove on his lap and a bottle of Monongahela at his elbow. She was running her fingers through his hair and whispering the naughty things she'd like to do with him when a harsh voice intruded on his daydream.

"Where do you reckon you're goin', mister?"

Fargo snapped his head up and drew rein. "What the hell?"

There were two of them. Hard cases with six-shooters on their hips and suspicion in their eyes. Behind them were two horses. Neither the men nor their animals showed any sign of being withered by the sun.

"Can't you read?" the same man said, pointing.

Fargo looked and blinked. "I must be sunstruck."

Someone had planted a sign. In painted letters it read: INFERNO SALT LICK. TRESPASSERS WILL BE SHOT.

"Move along, mister," the second curly wolf said. "We won't tell you twice."

"My horse can use some water. There must be some hereabouts."

The first man stuck his thumbs in his gun belt. He wore a high-crowned hat and a vest that could have used a cleaning. "Maybe there is, and maybe there ain't. Turn that nag and light a shuck."

"I asked nice," Fargo said.

The second man gestured at hills to the north. "You see yonder? That's the lick. There's a spring. But Mr. Crillian, who runs things, doesn't let anybody take a drink except him and those who work for him."

"Which would be us," the first man said.

"If you want water," the second man said, and gestured to the east, "Inferno is about five miles thataway."

"Inferno?"

The man in the high-crowned hat snickered. "You have no notion of where you are, do you, buckskin?"

"Daniel Boone, here, must be lost, Clell," the second man joked.

Excerpt from SIX-GUN INFERNO

"Dumb as a stump, Willy," Clell said.

They laughed.

Fargo's gaze fell on their horses and on what was hanging from their saddle horns. "How much for one of your canteens?"

"They ain't for sale," Clell said. "Mosey on, or else."

"I'll pay you twenty dollars for one," Fargo offered.

"You don't listen too good, mister," Willy said. "You're not gettin' any water. You're on private property, and you've been told to scat."

"So scat," Clell said.

Fargo sighed. He looked at the blue sky and at the two guards and at the Ovaro wearily hanging its head. Before the men could guess his intent, he swung down and took a step to one side, his hand brushing his holster. "Thirty-one dollars, but that's all I have."

Clell and Willy couldn't seem to believe their eyes.

"What does it take to get through that thick skull of yours?" Clell said.

"We want you gone, mister," Willy said. "We want you gone *now*."

"My horse needs water," Fargo said again.

"Tough," Willy said. "You can't make us give you any—not if we don't want to."

"Which we don't," Clell said. "Your critter can keel over, for all I care. Climb back on and make yourself scarce."

Fargo had no right to do what he was about to do. But he was prickly where the Ovaro was concerned. Plus, he never could abide jackasses. "Either I pay you, or I help myself. Your choice."

"Try and you die," Willy warned. "We'll give you to the count of three, and then we will by-God gun you if you're not back on that animal of yours." He paused and, when Fargo didn't move, barked out, "One."

"To hell with that," Clell said. "You don't need to count. I'll settle his hash, here and now." So saying, he stabbed for his six-gun.

No other series packs this much heat!

THE TRAILSMAN

Follow the trail of Penguin's Action Westerns at
penguin.com/actionwesterns

National bestselling author
RALPH COMPTON

"A writer in the tradition of Louis L'Amour and Zane Grey!" —*Huntsville Times*

Available wherever books are sold or at
penguin.com

S543

THE LAST OUTLAWS

The Lives and Legends of Butch Cassidy and the Sundance Kid

by Thom Hatch

Butch Cassidy and the Sundance Kid are two of the
most celebrated figures of American lore. As leaders of
the Wild Bunch, also known as the Hole-in-the-Wall
Gang, they planned and executed the most daring
bank and train robberies of the day, with an
uprecedented professionalism.

The Last Outlaws brilliantly brings to life these
thrilling, larger-than-life personalities like never before,
placing the legend of Butch and Sundance in the
context of a changing—and shrinking—American
West, as the rise of 20th century technology brought
an end to a remarkable era. Drawing on a wealth of
fresh research, Thom Hatch pushes aside the myth and
offers up a compelling, fresh look at these icons of the
Wild West.